MW00583441

Richard Matheson was b[...]
in 1926 and grew up in Br[...]
began at an early age: his first published work, a poem, appeared when he
was eight, and as a teen he read voraciously. After graduating from high
school, Matheson served in the army during World War II, an experience
that would form the basis for his novel *The Beardless Warriors* (1960). Following his military service, Matheson studied journalism at the University
of Missouri and began to devote himself to writing.

Matheson first gained widespread exposure and notice with a story
published in *The Magazine of Fantasy and Science Fiction* in 1950, "Born of
Man and Woman," about a husband and wife who give birth to a monster
which they keep hidden in a cellar. It would go on to become the title
story of his first collection, which appeared in 1954 during a period of
extraordinary creative fertility that also produced several classic novels,
I Am Legend (1954), *The Shrinking Man* (1956), and *A Stir of Echoes* (1958).
Over the course of his long career, Matheson would go on to publish
some two-dozen novels and numerous short stories in a variety of genres,
including horror, fantasy, suspense, paranormal, science fiction and, later
in life, westerns, including *Journal of the Gun Years*, winner of the Spur
Award for Best Western Novel.

Matheson was also a prolific screenwriter for television and film. His
television credits include many of the best-loved episodes of *The Twilight
Zone*, as well as popular series like *The Alfred Hitchcock Hour* and *Star Trek*,
and *The Night Stalker* (1972), the highest-rated television film of its time.
His film scripts include a number of classic Edgar Allan Poe adaptations,
as well as screenplays based on his own novels and stories for such films as
Duel (1971, directed by Steven Spielberg), *The Legend of Hell House* (1973),
and *Somewhere in Time* (1980). More recently, Matheson's works have
provided the basis for numerous films, including *What Dreams May Come*
(1998), *Stir of Echoes* (1999), and *I Am Legend* (2007).

In addition to his fiction, Matheson was a professional songwriter and
also published works on matters of the spiritual and metaphysical, including *The Path* (1993) and *A Primer of Reality* (2002).

His many awards include both the World Fantasy and Bram Stoker
awards for lifetime achievement, the Edgar Award and multiple Writers
Guild Awards, and he was inducted into the Science Fiction Hall of Fame
in 2010. He died in 2013.

RICHARD MATHESON

UNCOLLECTED STORIES

Edited by
WILLIAM F. NOLAN

Introduction by
DAVID J. SCHOW

Afterword by the Author

VALANCOURT BOOKS

Offbeat: Uncollected Stories
First published by Subterranean Press in 2002
This edition first published 2017

Published by Valancourt Books, Richmond, Virginia
http://www.valancourtbooks.com

ISBN 978-1-943910-64-9 (trade paperback)
Also available in ebook and audiobook formats

All Valancourt Books publications are printed on acid free paper that
meets all ANSI standards for archival quality paper.

Cover by Henry Petrides
Set in Dante MT

Contents

INTRODUCTION

Matheson, Senior

I HAVE FORGOTTEN WHETHER it was an article or editorial or introduction, but many years ago I once wrote a piece furiously stumping *I Am Legend* as one of the two most critically fundamental vampire novels of the 20th century; my other choice was Leslie Whitten's much more obscure *Progeny of the Adder*. This pair of ground-breakers did the heavy lifting, modernizing the mythos of the bloodsucker and providing a sturdy foundation for every derivative work that followed. There are other classics, sure; some arguably more popular, but none which did not bootstrap the writers who planted the flag, who innovated rather than recycled—and who got there first.

Richard Matheson had a knack for that kind of thing: simple prescience, and a common sense approach to the "single aberrant idea" that made him a mainstay go-to scenarist for Rod Serling. The twist, the potent "what-if." The essence of a Matheson tale is the oft-cited "ordinary people in extraordinary circumstances" springboard; everything is recognizable except for that one little nudge that skews the story into nightmare territory. Call it *Twilight Zone* thinking.

Along with his cohort and brother-from-another-mother Charles Beaumont, Matheson helped to gift an entire generation of eager drive-in customers with a refreshed Edgar Allan Poe canon.

The Matheson landmarks and accomplishments are legion, and you don't need me to cite chapter and verse. His influence was global. He remains a titan.

So whether you call it science fiction, or horror, or fantasy doesn't matter all that much, when what we're talking about here is plain, damned good writing, reliably delivered, decade after decade.

I was a total stranger when I first contacted Richard, by mail, seeking simple-minded biographical data so I could cobble together an entry on him for an encyclopedia called *The Fantasy Almanac*, by Jeff Rovin (Dutton, 1979). He surprised me by responding with a hand-written letter detailing his lineage and family—directly from the pen of the man himself!

"Richard Burton Matheson was born in 1926 in Allendale, New Jersey, the son of Bertolf Mathieson and Fanny Svengningsen, both of Oslo, Norway. A 1949 graduate of the University of Missouri (taking a degree in journalism), Matheson's first sale was the short story 'Born of Man and Woman' (later the title of his first collection), which was published in The Magazine of Fantasy & Science Fiction *in 1950 . . ."*

. . . and so on. He was twenty-four years old when he made that sale, and had already sweated out World War Two as an infantryman. Insert brief pause here, so you may reflect upon what you were doing at that age, what your aspirations or accomplishments might have been. Now imagine a world where you cannot Google this data instantly, that it may feel more special to you, as it did to me.

Many of his novels stand as benchmarks of their respective categories to this day—Matheson was, after all, the writer who tried to beat Shirley Jackson at her own game with *Hell House*—but it was his short fiction that particularly enthralled me during a time when I began to attempt the very same discipline myself. To this day, short stories don't get the respect of the "heavies"—novels—and I am frequently compelled to remind people that once upon a time, when Beaumont published in *Playboy* or Bradbury had a new tale in the *Saturday Evening Post*, damned near everybody was talking about that story the next day, at the lunch counter or 'round the water cooler.

The accepted wisdom of the times was that one broke ice with short fiction; then, if luck or taste prevailed, a nascent writer might step up to novel-length in a time-consuming, counter-intuitive, lock-stepped fashion that was just *the way things were done*, in the glacial timeline of publishing.

Matheson blew that thinking away by competently producing not only fiction short and long-form, but teleplays and screenplays as well, becoming one of the very few writers who could adroitly juggle *all* forms. As influence, he quickly became omnipresent.

It was in the early 1990s, while a flurry of Richard's Westerns (old and new) were flowering to a fresh audience, that he resurrected a project titled *7 Steps to Midnight*. Our mutual publisher at the time sent along an advance proof of this "new" Matheson novel, which upon reading seemed a bit more *vintage* to me. Sure enough: its first iteration had been ten years earlier, when Matheson was touring Europe; his itinerary had become his character's. But the astonishing part was that the publisher, seemingly tone-deaf, requested that I provide a blurb for the book. I had just published my first novel and was staggered by the sheer *wrongness* of the purported need for a new book by no less than The Matheson to be shilled by the likes of me—if anything, the flipside rule applied; my work stood to benefit far more from a Matheson quotation. The situation was so embarrassing that I never asked him for sell copy, ever.

A year or two later, I got invited to dinner, instead.

Joe Lansdale was along for that ride (Joe was visiting L.A., staying at my apartment at the time) as well as Richard Christian Matheson, whom I have now known for so long that I can't remember a world without him in it. After dessert we repaired to my Hollywood rathole, where I was subjected to the surreal sight of Richard Matheson himself, checking out my library and pulling books while making little humming noises. (I have never been prouder, or more relieved, by already having an entire Matheson shelf). He plucked my Gold Medal paperback edition of *I Am Legend* from its fellows and kindly inscribed it to me. Later—*later*, when I could afford more pricey hardcovers, I dutifully accumulated a few more signatures, autographs, inscriptions, the byproduct of subsequent get-togethers versus other favored titles, but I still have that little softcover with the unmistakable aroma of foxed paper, and it's a personal treasure, a souvenir of that bygone time.

Across the ensuing years we encountered each other many more times, and there was always the dispensation of being treated not as another reader or fan, but (as Robert Bloch once put it) as a "colleague."

Now *that* is empowering and encouraging.

Richard died, as our fathers and icons do, leaving us with the burden and duty of encomia. This is where it gets tricky. Hyperbole for the dead is too facile, too easy, and more or less inevitable once a career is celebrated posthumously. But I know that Richard was notoriously critical of much of his work—particularly adaptations made from it—and would scoff at or dismiss many of the adjectives tossed around too freely in his wake. It follows therefore that not every entry was a masterwork or brilliant classic, since that umbrella denies the sense of exploration, experimentation, and yes, occasional failure that denotes a lifetime invested in the pursuit of good storytelling.

Yet at the same time, the hazard of under-sell looms threateningly, when assessing the status of an celebrated figure. Statistics can (and will) be cited until your eyes bleed.

Offbeat—back in print following a hiatus of about a decade and a half—presents (for the most part) the younger Richard on the rise, still making his bones, ever-experimenting. You can read Richard's own Afterword for pedigree.

Among those refugee tales presented here (like the exhibits in "Relics"; please remember to keep your children in line) are:

"And Now I'm Waiting"—the source material for one of my very favorite *Twilight Zone* episodes was the outright horror tale (seen here) which evolved into a comedy for TV. It was still unpublished when the episode made from it ("A World All His Own") was broadcast as the season one closer to the series. It was also, as Matheson himself noted, "the only *TZ* episode in which one of the characters broke in on Rod's final narration and altered it!"

"And Now I'm Waiting" first saw print in the eponymous *Rod Serling's The Twilight Zone Magazine* in 1983, as did "Blunder Buss" the following year—another tale that shows Matheson's lighter side to advantage.

"Relics" (first appeared in *Cemetery Dance* #31, 1999) is another of Matheson's delicious black-as-pitch ruminations that coils back on itself from where you think it *might* have been going.

"The Prisoner"'s first publication was as a 2001 Gauntlet Press chapbook whose cover illustration was rendered by a friend and ally of mine, Marcelo "Buddy" Martinez (1962-2009), one of the progenitors of the short-lived *Iniquities* Magazine ... which no doubt would have brought new Matheson to the world had it survived beyond three issues. "The Prisoner" tackles another of Matheson's favorite topics, blurred identity, in a scenario that deliberately evokes Edgar Allan Poe's "The Pit and the Pendulum" ... until it plunges into a dark, a science-fictional detour.

"Always Before Your Voice" was a trunk story Matheson resurrected on behalf of *California Sorcery* (ed. William F. Nolan & William Schafer, Cemetery Dance, 1999)—another mainstream tale about frustration and desire, written in 1954 while he was writing *The Shrinking Man* in a rented house on Long Island.

How many baseball stories did Matheson write? Answer: *one*, and you'll find it here as "Maybe You Remember Him."

Intrepid Matheson bibliographers searching in vain for a story titled "All and Only Silence" will find it here under its original title, "The Last Blah in the Etc."

"Two O'Clock Session" was written for inclusion in a Ray Bradbury tribute volume, *The Bradbury Chronicles* (ed. William F. Nolan & Martin H. Greenberg, ROC, 1991). Nobody-but-nobody working in the realm of fantastic fiction from the 1950s onward was able to escape the Bradbury influence, including members of Matheson's own Green Hand and the Group. In the late 1990s, Matheson claimed a personal moratorium on writing short fiction "since 1970." Here, he is back at full strength, refreshed and ready to deliver a short, sharp shock not unlike those that became the stock in trade of his son, Richard Christian.

So, full circle: after nearly thirty years since being asked, here I am, blurbing Richard Matheson at last, with what I hope is at least a passing mock of humility.

This is what I take away: Richard Matheson was a friend. His uncommon kindness and (often-invisible) generosity was a real basis for genuine respect. And the reason we do books such as this one is to keep him alive in our hearts. It is up to the reader to judge whether we have honored his legacy to a standard that Richard himself might have appreciated. He might have even made one of those little humming noises.

David J. Schow
December 2016

Special thanks to John Scoleri for all things Matheson.

DAVID J. SCHOW is a multiple-award-winning writer who lives in Los Angeles. The latest of his nine novels is a hardboiled extravaganza called

The Big Crush (2017). The newest of his nine short story collections is a monster-fest titled *DJSturbia* (2016). He has written extensively for film (*The Crow, Leatherface: Texas Chainsaw Massacre III, The Hills Run Red*) and television (*Masters of Horror, Mob City*). One of *Fangoria* magazine's most popular columnists, he is also the world's foremost authority on a terribly obscure 1960s TV series, *The Outer Limits*. As editor he has curated both Robert Bloch (*The Lost Bloch*, three volumes, 1999-2002) and John Farris (*Elvisland*, 2004) as well as assembling the legendary anthology *Silver Scream* (1988). His recent nonfiction works include *The Art of Drew Struzan* (2010) and *The Outer Limits at 50* (2014). He can be seen on various DVDs as expert witness or documentarian on everything from *Creature from the Black Lagoon* and *Psycho* to *I, Robot* and *King Cohen: The Wild World of Filmmaker Larry Cohen*. Thanks to him, the word "splatterpunk" has been in the Oxford English Dictionary since 2002.

OFFBEAT

For all the good Mathesons, for all the good years.

Relics

THE SUN HADN'T MADE A MOVE ALL MORNING.
It was hiding behind a thick carpet of clouds that was stretched over the sky. Waves of damp chilling wind swept over the sidewalks as the little group marched in scattered formation.

Her eyes roamed listlessly over the ranks of her pupils.

Already she was exhausted and they hadn't even gone into the museum yet. She lifted her gaze and looked at the massive grey building they approached.

"Stay together!" she ordered for what seemed the hundredth time.

She wanted to strangle all the little boys for running into the streets and hiding behind trees and popping out to frighten the little girls. She wanted to strangle the little girls for shrieking in delight when it happened. Be a teacher, Mother told me, she thought, overwhelmed by irritation.

The pupils bunched together momentarily and hurried on across the wide square. As they reached the building, they flung themselves up the wide marble steps in a frontal attack on the entrance.

"Stay together!" she howled after them.

She hurried up the steps and swished through the door. The children were dispersed and ogling in the high-ceilinged lobby. She flew about, huddling them in a mass like a herder flocking sheep.

"You'll all stop this nonsense or back to school we'll go," she threatened breathlessly as she counted heads and glared at innocent blandness.

They were all present.

3

"Now stay here," she ordered, "I'm going to look at the directory."

She started away, turned. "Don't move!"

In front of the high white-lettered directory she stood breathing heavily.

"Children," she muttered, scanning the words. *Reptiles*, she read with her lips and thought of the children again. The prospect of the long maddening ride ahead, back to the school made her groan inside. Her eyes flitted over the letters.

Behind her came the sound of someone flopping soundly on the floor. She turned, jade-eyed, to see what new outrages were being committed.

The army had cracked.

Three boys ran a furious game of *Catch Me Catch Me* around a case of ancient beadwork.

Two girls stood far across the lobby speaking to the attendant at the souvenir stand.

Two other boys were making a serious attempt to pry up a tile with their knives.

The rest were drifting about like hawser-cut ships in erratic currents.

She groaned deeply and rushed over the dark floor. Angrily she dragged up the two probers and shook them. Her urgent hiss sped to the three boys skidding around the exhibit case. They scuffed back into the tightening group, cringing under her cold-eyed surveillance.

"Stay. Together," she said. She turned away and moved toward the stand.

The two little girls turned as she approached.

"We were just asking," one of them said timidly.

"I told you to stay with the *what are you pointing at?*"

She looked around and her mouth dropped.

"You just *went* a little while ago," she snapped.

"I have to again," said the little girl.

She slumped in disgusted weariness. Go one, go all, she thought. "Pity's sake," she droned.

She bought a guide book before escorting the girls back to the restless assemblage.

"How many have to, I say *have to* go to the bathroom?" she inquired.

All of them. Why do I bother asking? she thought, they'll probably get more enjoyment out of flushing toilets than they do out of all the centuries on display.

A weary pied piper of the glands, she led them across the lobby. She dropped off the little boys with a harsh gestured reminder that they absolutely had to be back in the hall in five minutes, no more. She watched them fly through the swinging door like a charging herd of horses. Inside, the muffled whoops and giggles of lifted restraint billowed high.

She grunted in submission and ushered the girls through the next entrance down.

Inside the anteroom she sank down on a seat and moaned. She looked, half asleep, at the opposite wall. The guide book slipped from her grasp and thumped on the floor.

She didn't budge or speak or nod even when the two little girls began screeching at each other and another one came bursting out of the bathroom to report a battle royal.

At long last they were reassembled; like pieces of a vibrating machine that kept flying apart.

She counted heads. All there. She pointed toward the animal hall directly at the head of the lobby and followed the tide of them as they moved forward.

The children hopped and skipped and jumped through the hall entrance.

"Walk right!" she specified in teeth-grinding belligerence. They filed into the hall as penitent as a line of monks.

She looked at the words over the doorway as she passed beneath.

George East Hall, the letters spelled.

George East. She consulted the shelves of her memory. George East had been a famous explorer. Long ago. She recalled reading a book of his once when she was a child. *Trapping Big Game in Africa*. That was the title, she recalled, smiling pensively at a reflection of youth past.

Inside, she had to blink several times before she could see at all. It was like entering a mosque or, at least, a darkened theater. It smelled like a mosque.

The only lights were in the glass-enclosed exhibits on each side of the hall that flowed away into a shadowy blur.

She was struck by the sudden cessation of sound from her pupils. They talked in solemn muted tones and, even those who could not restrain their giggles, throttled them rather effectively. In a church, in a museum, she thought; where it is dark and reeks of all things old, the children and the grown act like this; as if the darkness were something sacred in itself, not to be violated.

The children were gazing into the first exhibit.

She tried to read the guide book but it was too dark for that. She went up to the plastiglass front and leaned forward to read the descriptive metal plate on the wall.

"Children, this is the Water Buffalo," she said, rattling off the description.

She glanced at them after her reading. They looked apathetic. They weren't listening, she thought, and her mouth assumed a betrayed fixity. Well, why should I try then? she thought. Why should I go blind for pity's sake when they don't even care. I won't, she decided; that's all.

Thinking militant thoughts, she stared in at the stuffed and posed animals. It was well done, she managed to appreciate despite her peeve.

They seemed almost alive, frozen in time, ready at the touch of a wand to go on with their battle.

She tried to imagine that; tried to visualize the thick hooves spraying the hot musky air with black soil, the green-surfaced pool splattering water up their heaving flanks, the air ringing with the clash of their saber horns.

Impossible, she concluded. How could I possibly imagine it? The dead are dead.

Into her ears slipped a whisper apparently meant to be secretive but which echoed. What is noisier than a child trying to be quiet? she thought, glancing aside in slowly churning anger.

The pupils had drifted again, the structure of her class shattered. The parts were stretched out over the next four exhibits.

Her hiss vibrated in the air like the warning of a truculent viper. They all recognized her distinctive summons and came back pettishly to take their places in the group again.

"For pity's sake, stay together!" she commanded, her voice rising with a passion. "Stop wandering around without my permission!"

"May I only go and . . ."

"Stay together!" she groaned, her voice frayed to a string. Stay together. The words collapsed in her mind. She had to concentrate for a long moment to remember what they meant.

She stopped before the next exhibit, standing behind all of them so none could make a getaway.

"That's an elephant," she announced with bellicose assurance.

"Rhinoceros," corrected a little boy loudly. "It says."

She cleared her throat, vaguely wishing that the rhinoceros would plunge out through the glass plate and trample the little boy to a grease spot.

"That's right," she amended, "I'm glad to see that one of you, at least, is awake when I test your observance."

She glared menacingly at the charging black-hided monster whose ears stood eternally on end and whose nostrils would be flaring until the trumpet blew.

For a brief moment she tried to imagine again. She tried to hear the thunder of the hoofs, the crackling of the grasses.

Impossible. She kicked it aside. Why bother trying to resurrect something never even known?

"Let's go to the next one," she said in a tired voice, the vision of acres and acres of exhibits creeping disconcertingly into her mind. The groan in her was audible only to those children closest to her and it was nothing strange to them.

They went down the hall and across the hall and up the hall and in and out all the hall's side extensions. They looked at lions and elephants and gazelles and zebras and giraffes and wildebeests. To her it seemed as if they looked at everything George East had ever come across in his life including fungus and his first wife.

She got sick of stuffed immobility. What are they anyway? she thought. Relics of a past so dead that it's worthy of nothing but strict privacy.

These things were no longer interesting to her or the children or anyone. Fleshed or unfleshed, they were just heaps of bone that would never never move again.

Now they were away from George East's taxidermied exploits, back in the lobby.

She ached. She wanted to sit down and call it a day for the rest of the year.

But I can't, she thought. I have to plunge on with this hellish safari through the halls of the better forgotten. It was her job. No one cared. Not really. But here they were and they had to go through with it.

They all flooded into the next wing like raging water seeking its level. I have never in my entire life, she thought, seen a weary child. I think that I could die happy if I could only be assured that children do get tired sometime, anytime.

Deep Sea Fish, read the huge lettered sign sagging a trifle lopsided on the wall.

She didn't care. She looked with complete disinterest at the stripe-bellied whale stretching half the length of the hall. She gazed in patient apathy at the crescent-mouthed shark gobbling up his neighbors. She looked up wearily as she passed under the huge grotesque turtle straddling the air over her.

The children didn't care either. They glanced at, passed over, ignored; always rushing on, flashing to the next case, the next room, the next wing. As long as they can move and move and move, that's all that matters, she thought.

At odd moments, she tried to tighten up their columns. Mostly she let them wander.

She stood before it.

It was long and tarnished and it looked like a gigantic bullet from some long ago conflict.

It was opened, cut lengthwise as though severed cleanly with a lone blow.

Next to it was a huge glass case. Various articles were arranged in the case. They had all been taken out of the metal shell once. It said so on the plate.

She looked at the cards under each article and read about it in the guide book.

Makeup kit, read the card. *For the face*, explained the guide book.

Watch. (*For chronological computation*) *Tobacco*. (*A primordial vice*) *Golf tees*. (*An element of another primordial vice*) *Lock and key*. (*For protecting of valuables*) *Toothbrush and powder*. (*For the teeth*)

She shook her head and glanced aside to see if her tribe was on the warpath. They were widely dispersed but otherwise behaved. She looked back at the case.

Shaving Kit. Football Rules. $1. 50¢. 25¢. 10¢. 5¢. 1¢.

She didn't bother reading the explanations for these things. She didn't care what they signified. If they signified anything, she thought.

She glanced down at a brown-edged magazine. *Life*, it read. She looked at the face of a man long dead and gone, smiling up from the cover.

"Errol Flynn," she said, testing the sound of the words. She shrugged then. No matter.

For the face, for the teeth, a primordial vice, a primordial vice element, football rules.

She sighed. What a sad lot, she thought. These people were a sorry heap of pettiness and hauteur.

She turned away from the case. She rounded up her herd.

"Come on children," she said. "We're leaving this room now."

Another hall. It smelled a little cleaner. It was a little more modern; if you considered all things modern that were under two thousand years old.

She consulted the guide book, shifting her weight in tired movements.

"Automobiles," she read to herself, "common vehicles in the twentieth through the thirty-sixth centuries."

She looked over the book top at the flimsy sagging structure. It looked pathetic compared to present achievement, she decided.

It was yellow and it had only four wheels and the seats inside were, of all things, covered with the hides of animals that were as dead as everything else.

She looked at the stained metal parts, ran an examining touch over the dried up glass that she supposed had been designed to keep the wind from those who sat attempting to steer with that odd thick spoked wheel angling up from the cracked floorboards.

"Oh my," she muttered to herself, unable to appreciate the quaintness of outmoded custom.

She turned away from it and looked at her dispersed army with a slight moan. She moved about, consolidating and ordering, brought up to the solid present by the necessity of preventing her charges from tearing down the building.

Floor by floor, they moved, higher and higher. Through an endless array of dim halls, wide stretches of assembled bone meant, it appeared, to remind someone long ago that something called a dinosaur once was affluent if now it was just a wired junk heap.

Rooms and chambers and halls and miles of display that smelled of the ancient. Cases and cases of pottery, glasswork, gems, machines, cars. "Everlasting laid out corpses," she said to herself, "made of bone and stone and crusted steel."

They were on another floor. She forgot which one it was. She'd lost track of them. It seemed she'd been climbing stairs all her life and the next flight would lead to heaven.

They were moving through a great somber hall. The children's voices fluttered up like frail bats and were lost in the massy silence. Soon it has to be over, she thought, they can't make this building much higher.

She moved to the wall and slumped down on a seat. Her eyes moved wearily to the center of the room.

A great silvery coated rocket ship stood there, fenced in and motionless, its stubby nose pointing toward the sky. Only the ceiling blocked the sky away and there was something depressing in the sight of the silvery ship walled in forever.

She flipped open the guide book. There was a small illustration of the ship. *Luna I. First Ship to Reach the Moon*, read the picture caption.

"How nice," she muttered, bored, glancing aside as a little girl came up to her.

"Are we going to eat soon?" asked the little girl.

"As soon as we finish on this floor," she decided all at once. The little girl went away, skipping.

She leaned against the wall. It's hot in here, she thought, closing her eyes. Hot and stuffy and weary. A museum is a hot stale shell of information. She nodded and snapped back to attention, her eyes opened wide and peering at the silent ship.

"All old things are funny."

She said it to herself and they were. Spacesuits and rocket engines and guided missiles and atom bombs. They were all funny and old and useless.

For a moment she slipped into the first moment of peaceful reverie she had managed to effect all day. It was pleasant to forget, eyes closed and body limp.

Then, abruptly, her eyes swept open and the old beset expression narrowed her face.

Two boys were wrestling on the floor.

She got up with a hiss of rage and hurried over to them.

"Stop it!" she snapped in a rage, dragging them up from tumbling combat, "Don't you have any sense at all?"

The boys eyed each other with sullen threatening expressions.

"Yeah, well, I'll get you," said one to the other.

"One more outbreak like this and I'll send a nice long note to your parents," she threatened. "Would you like that?"

They looked up hastily.

"*Would* you?"

"No," they said. They both shook their heads.

"Then behave," she ordered. "Pity's sake. Always this fighting, fighting. Don't you ever learn?"

They started into the last room on the floor, a little room tucked away in one corner.

Another girl mentioned hunger and they all murmured restively.

"As soon as we finish here!" she said.

"Yay!" said the boys.

"Quiet!" she said. "Now go look around. And, just for once, appreciate all this wonderful knowledge kept here for you." She looked for another bench.

There weren't any. So she moved around the room. The children were all sweeping around like windblown leaves, glancing once at each case and rushing on. Some of them were back at the door already, waiting for the descent to the cafeteria.

"Well, *look* at things," she muttered angrily under her breath.

She stood obdurately in front of a case, determined to read every word on the placard before she budged back to the class.

She gazed in irritated disdain at the exhibit in the case. What a sorry sight, she thought. Her gaze moved down.

Homo Sapiens. Man, read the plate. *Bulk of species destroyed after invasion of Earth in year 4726.*

Now extinct.

She looked back. They were assembled tightly, all by themselves; driven to a desperate orderliness by their appetites.

"Oh, I give up," she groaned, moving back to them.

And, as they started out, she spoke again, half to them and half to herself.

"We're not staying after lunch either," she said. "There's nothing in the rest of the museum anyway but more dead animals."

Blunder Buss

IT WAS THE THOUSANDTH DAY. He had started in September of 1952, and here it was, June of '55. He had counted the days, making tiny checks on a piece of paper he kept in his wallet.

A thousand days in love with Marilyn Taylor.

For the thousandth time he slipped the cover over his adding machine, plucked off his cellophane cuffs, and locked up his desk. He was in the office but he was really in Hollywood immersed in a fancy, wallowing in cinemascopic delights. Instinct alone put the coat over his sparse frame, the Panama on his semi-bald skull. Habit took him to the elevator, out the main door of the Lane Building, and down the steps into the steamy dimness of the subway, where he was shoehorned into the heat-laden train by a horde of nine-to-fivers. He hardly felt the bony elbows, though, the grunts of agony, the snarled complaints.

Henry Shrivel was dreaming.

The thousandth day. That was a record. Never had such love been so faithful, he thought as he swayed with the motion of the train. Sweat dripped off his face as he thought of her.

Then, two stations after he'd gotten on, the mass of people wedged him further into the car. He grabbed a vacant strap and slipped back into reverie. The train was halfway across the bridge before his eyes lighted on the advertisement at his left. His mouth popped open, his pale blue eyes grew wide.

It was Her.

She was standing on a tennis court smiling fondly at a cigarette which she held in the V of her two shapely fingers. Her eyes peered into Henry Shrivel's soul.

"Charnel Cigarettes," she was commenting, "are milder and tastier. They are my brand." Signed: "Marilyn Taylor, Classic Studios. Now appearing in *The Karamazov Boys*."

Henry Shrivel gazed adoringly at her. Her hair was blond and fluffy. Her eyes were cat green, sultry, inviting him to blood-curdling pleasures. Her scarlet lips implored to be taken.

The illustration was cut off where the line of her shoulders began the inexorable slope into her internationally famed bosom. Hollywood's most lavish bust; the columnists had voted her that signal honor. And, oh, 'tis true, 'tis true, thought Henry Shrivel as he hung glassy-eyed from the subway strap.

All the way home he watched her standing on the tennis court, cool, unruffled, frozen in beauty. *"Marilyn is quite the tennis player." Screen Magazine* had said it. She must be; here was incontrovertible evidence.

Suddenly a bolt of prescience struck Henry Shrivel square between the eyes. It was a sign, a most definite sign. A clear indication that tonight his efforts would be crowned with success.

Tonight he would hold Marilyn Taylor in his arms.

He got off at the last stop and walked slowly up the steps onto the noisy avenue. He stepped lightly over the trolley tracks, ignoring the taxicab which almost knocked him down. Slowly he strolled away from the noise, turned a corner, and started up the quiet, tree-lined street. The thousandth day, he thought.

Or—to be explicit—the thousandth *night*.

It was muggy in the apartment. It smelled of boiled cabbage and drying diapers. For the moment, Henry Shrivel forced reality into his mind. For the last time he would play the role of doting spouse.

Bella was in the kitchen ladling pabulum into the gurgling

baby. Hair stringed down over Bella's forehead and temples; there was sweat on her gaunt features. Marilyn Taylor would never look like that, he thought; no, not even in *this* apartment.

"Hello," he said.

"Oh," she said, "It's you." She raised a damp forehead, and reluctantly he brushed his lips across it. "You're late," she said.

You always say that, Henry thought, *even when I'm early.*

"Yes, dear," he said. "Are we eating soon?"

"I have to finish feeding Lana," Bella said. "Then I'll start supper."

"Oh, you haven't started yet."

"No, I haven't started yet! What do you think I've been doing all day—*loafing?* Why, I've been—"

Henry stood there patiently while she unraveled a spool of various complaints. "Yes, d—" he interposed once, but she wasn't finished. "Yes, dear," he repeated, when she had stated her case.

He went into the living room and opened a window to let the smell out. He kicked a wagon aside, threw Willie's basketball into the dining room, and picked up jigsaw pieces which were strewn all over the rug.

At length, with a sigh, he lowered himself onto the couch and sat there a few moments, breathing in inurement to his surroundings. Then he lay on his back and pressed his eyes shut. The room drifted away. He plied his secret.

In the beginning it had only been pretense, the release of imagining. But that was a thousand days ago. Now he believed it.

When he closed his eyes he was in Marilyn Taylor's bedroom.

"I'm on her bed," he whispered in his mind. "I can hear the drapes whispering as warm California breezes float through the tall French windows which open on the terrace which overlooks the free-form swimming pool which has gorgeous starlets sitting around it, flexing their golden bodies."

Henry Shrivel sighed. He had it down pat now. After a thousand nights—minus one—of mental positioning he was certain of it. Only one item remained. He had to kiss Marilyn Taylor. That was the cachet. Just kiss her.

And then...

Yes. He could actually *feel* the room around him now. He knew every detail of it, he'd seen it from so many angles in the movie magazines—the magazines he'd scoffed at when Bella stacked them around the apartment, but which he pored over, devoured, all the while pretending that he was looking down his nose at them.

He knew Marilyn Taylor's house as well as he knew his own apartment. The shelves of book-club selections in the paneled library, the parabolic couch sprawling in front of the vast fieldstone fireplace in the living room, the hi-fidelity equipment, the spongy rugs, the chairs and tables, the lamps. The sparkling chrome and copper kitchen where Marilyn posed in lacy aprons making biscuits. *"Marilyn is quite the cook." Fanland Magazine* had said it.

Every night for a thousand nights less one he had projected himself into that house, walked around it, lay on her bed, waiting for her.

"I am on Marilyn's bed," he whispered again. "I've just had a hard set of tennis with her. I've already taken my shower and I'm lying here without my clothes on. In the bathroom I can hear the water spattering over her body. I can hear her squealing in delight as the streams of bubbles snake over her bronzed flesh."

Henry shriveled on the couch. It was there! He could sense it, feel it, hear it.

And why not? Time and space—what were they really? Elastic media subject to personal expansion and contraction. If a man concentrated long enough *anything* was possible.

"Soon the shower will be turned off. She will toss a thick terrycloth robe over her wet body. Like the one she wore in *Corpse on the Beach*. She will come gliding out of the bathroom and smile at me, a sensuous smile. 'Why, Henry, honey,' she'll coo. She'll come to the bed. She'll sit beside me."

The scene gained more reality with every second. Tonight he knew he would actually feel the bed yielding to her lissome weight, feel her fingers caressing his cheek. "You're such a handsome rogue," she'd say, and he'd really hear her say it. *Really*.

He'd keep his eyes shut, of course. She'd beg for a kiss as she had nine hundred and ninety-nine times before. Only this time—this thousandth night—he'd wait until his brain powers were irresistible. Then he'd put his hands on her shoulders. He'd pull her down. He'd feel the swell of that fantastic bust against him. Then he'd kiss her, and he'd actually feel those satiny lips yielding to his.

"And then I'll open my eyes. And I won't be in the apartment anymore. I'll be in Hollywood with her, holding her. Really! The escape will be made. I'll be away from everything, with Marilyn Taylor in my arms. Sighing in ecstasy in my male embrace. And then—"

"Henry! Eat!"

The bubble burst. Henry Shrivel was catapulted back into his living room. He gritted his teeth and pounded his fists into the cushions. Dust scaled up into the air.

"Damn," he muttered under his breath. "Oh ... *double damn*."

He sat up. He picked up a movie magazine from the table next to the couch and flipped it open to a feature story about Her. She beamed at him over the handle of a vacuum cleaner. *"Marilyn is quite the housekeeper,"* said the caption. Henry Shrivel relaxed; he smiled. No need to fret. Tonight the break would be made. Tonight. Oh, blessed tonight.

★

At supper he was almost charitable.

He patted Willie on the head and inquired about the doings at P. S. 106. He kissed the baby's cheek with infinite tenderness. He clucked sympathetically at Bella's tirade about her feet, her legs, her back, her eyes, her teeth, her head, and anything else she felt inclined to complain about. All in all, he acted very much like the soldier on the eve of departure for the wars—gallant and definitely underplaying it. It was unfortunate that no one noticed it but him.

When the meal had ended, Henry complimented Bella on the excellence of the cuisine. This made her narrow her eyes into suspicious slits.

"You feel all right?" she asked.

"I feel wonderful," said Henry Shrivel.

She peered at him. A mild sense of alarm burst in his chest. Then he relaxed. Bella couldn't possibly suspect. It was all in the mind, where she couldn't reach him.

She stopped the visual inquisition after a while. But all night she glanced at him occasionally while they sat in the living room watching half-hour murder mysteries and reading movie magazines.

Henry deliberately avoided thinking about Marilyn Taylor all evening. He wanted to store up the longing. He just sat in his easy chair staring at the television set without seeing anything, thinking about what the neighbors would say when he was gone.

"Disappeared! Yes! That's what I said! Just like that! Went to bed and the next morning he was gone, pajamas and all! Not a sign of him! Yes! Swallowed up! No one knows what to make of it!"

Henry Shrivel smiled a secret smile.

Bedtime.

The moment drew nigh. Despite rigid control, Henry found his heart beating rapidly, his breaths coming fast.

While he brushed his teeth he noticed how his hands shook. Nothing to be nervous about, he told himself. This is what you've been working toward. Tonight you reap your harvest. You're going to make it, boy, you're going to make it!

His hands still shook.

When he went into the bedroom, Bella was just getting into bed, the faded blue nightgown hanging from her lean body. Henry Shrivel's lips trembled, his legs shook. He sat down quickly on the bed.

"Set the clock," said Bella.

"*Huh?* Oh. Yes, dear. I will." His voice was drawn and shaky.

"What's the matter with you?" Bella asked.

"Noth-ulp." He swallowed. "Nothing. Something in my throat, that's all."

"Oh. Well, goodnight."

He kissed her on the cheek. His body shook. He fell back on the pillow with a thump. Am I doing right? he wondered. Is it right I should leave her and the children like this? Will my small insurance be enough?

His face tightened. By George, he hadn't gone through all this mental strain to back down now. Not after nine hundred and ninety-nine days and nights of aching concentration. It was only fair he should be rewarded for all the work.

If worse came to worst, he conceded, he could always get a train back from Hollywood. But he was sure Marilyn would get him a movie contract playing character parts, and he could send anonymous checks to Bella. Sure!

He smiled and closed his eyes. He tensed his body, willed it over the miles. Almost instantly, he was there. He felt Marilyn's bedroom around him; no point in walking through the whole damned house *tonight*. He was in her bed. He heard the drapes whispering. Outside, the starlets laughed by the pool. It was still late afternoon out there. In the bathroom shower, he heard Marilyn squealing.

"Come out of the shower," he said.

"Wha'?" Bella asked, thickly.

Henry's eyes jerked open, his heart pounding. He caught his breath and lay there until he heard Bella snoring. Then he closed his eyes and fled back to Marilyn's bedroom. A great effort forced the surroundings into his mind's eye.

"Come out of the shower," he said again, this time in his mind.

He listened. Breath caught once more. There was no sound but that of the breeze through the windows, the distant laughter of the starlets.

There!

A door opened. He heard bare feet on the rug. It was clear, so clear.

"Why, Henry, honey."

He heard it! *Heard* it! His heart hammered against the wall of his chest. He gritted his teeth, but they kept chattering. The footsteps moved across the rug. His hands twitched at his sides. He almost screamed as the bed sank at his side. She was sitting by him! His shoes shook; his entire frame was covered by waves of heat.

A *hand caressed his cheek*. A real hand, a warm, sensually stroking hand. Henry Shrivel shook with a palsy.

"You're such a handsome rogue."

Her low, inviting voice filled his brain with delirium. She was there. He felt her hand, heard her voice, smelled the perfume of her body, her hair. Every sense proclaimed her presence.

"Kiss me, Henry honey," she said in a begging whisper.

Now. It was the test, the crucial moment of moments. If he was strong now he could have her always. Marilyn Taylor —*his*. He drew every cell of his body into a tight, resourceful mass. He fired willpower through his throbbing veins.

"*Kiss me,*" Marilyn begged.

Slowly, carefully, he raised his hands.

They closed over her shoulders, tightened. He began to pull her down slowly, with the utmost caution. Once she almost vaporized. He drove a stronger jolt of volition through his system. She returned. She was there, fully then.

Now he felt her gelatinous breasts against his chest. The perfume of her clouding breath intoxicated him. His body shivered uncontrollably as her warm lips closed over his, the mass of her silky hair cascaded over his cheeks. His arms slid around her. Her robe fell open, her body pressed against him. Abandon raged in Henry Shrivel's blood. He had succeeded!

He opened his eyes. Slight surprise made his brow contract. It wasn't afternoon, it was pitch black night. Well, no matter. She was still in his arms; he felt her there. They writhed and groaned in each other's embrace.

"What's going on?"

Light flooded suddenly into Henry Shrivel's face: He jolted to a sitting position, eyes wide with nerve-shattered shock. His open-mouthed stare flashed from Marilyn Taylor's startled expression to his other side—to Bella's gaping features, her look of absolute astonishment.

"Henry Shrivel!" she gasped. "*What's going on here!*"

"Yeah!" said Marilyn, "What the hell *is?*"

Henry sank back, goggling. The last thing he saw, before his eyes closed in a dead faint, was the ceiling of his own bedroom.

And Now I'm Waiting

M ARY LET ME IN as soon as I rang the bell. She must have been waiting in the hallway.

I'd never in my life seen my sister look so unhappy. Sorrow had woven lines into her face unnatural for her age. And although neatness was an ingrained habit, not even her hair was combed. It fell around her shoulders in tangled brown swirls.

I leaned over to kiss her cheek and felt how cool and dry it was.

"Give me your things," she said.

I took off my hat and coat and handed them to her. She put them in the hall closet. I noticed how her once straight shoulders were now bowed. I grew taut with anger at what he'd done to her.

Then a shiver ran through me. I realized it was almost as cold in the house as outside. I rubbed my hands together.

Then she was beside me.

"Mary," I said, and put my arms around her. I felt her shudder.

"Thank you for coming," she said. "I can't bear it anymore."

"Where is he?" I asked.

She hung onto me for a moment. Then she pulled away and looked toward the study.

"Alone?" I asked.

Her eyes avoided mine. She nodded once.

I took her hand again. "It'll be all right."

She lifted my hand and pressed it against her cheek. Then she turned away.

23

"Will you wait here?" I asked.

"All right, David," she said.

I watched her walk to a chair against the stairs. She sat down and folded her hands on her lap.

I turned and walked to the study door, stood before it a second. Then, taking a deep breath, I knocked.

"What is it?" he called impatiently.

"David," I said.

It was silent. Finally he said, "Oh, come in."

Richard was standing in front of the fireplace, a giant of a man. His back was turned to me. He was staring into the crackling flames, an aura of light outlining his powerful form, casting shadows of him on the walls and ceiling.

"What is it?" he said, without turning.

"Mary told me I'd find you here," I said.

"Clever," he said. "Is that all?"

I shut the door behind me.

He turned as I walked toward him, a familiar expression of arrogance on his handsome features.

"So Mary told you I was in here, did she?" he said.

I sat down on the couch facing him.

"I want to talk to you," I said.

He looked down at me, then turned away.

"Talk about what?" he said.

I twisted around and turned on a lamp on the table behind me.

"I don't want that lamp on," he said.

"I want to see what you look like."

He turned around again. I felt a shudder run down my back as his icy eyes looked into mine. His lips drew back in a contemptuous smile.

"Do I pass?" he said. "Are you satisfied?"

"You're not as I'd expected," I said.

"Or as Mary led you to expect."

"She said only—"

"I can imagine what she said," he interrupted. "Turn off that lamp."

I reached back and turned it off. Once more his shadow billowed on the walls and ceiling.

"You look ill," I told him.

"Come twenty miles to tell me that?"

He stretched out his arms and rested them across the top of the fireplace. For a brief moment, I had the sensation that I was watching some ancient monarch in his hunting lodge.

"No, I didn't come twenty miles to tell you that," I said. "You know why I came."

"She sent for you," he said.

My fingers shook as I took out my cigarettes and lit one. I hoped he wouldn't notice.

"That's beside the point," I said. "Suppose you tell me what's wrong."

"You haven't answered my question," he said.

"Yes," I said, "she sent for me. I'm surprised she waited so long."

"Surprised?"

"Mary is about to have a nervous breakdown," I said.

"Oh," he said, "I see."

"You don't see at all," I said. "You don't *care* at all."

"Care!" he cried in a burst of temper. "How many nights have I sat with her trying to explain, trying to reason with a ... block of wood!" He clenched his fists. "But who can explain that—"

He broke off the sentence and walked to a shadowy portion of the room. I heard him drop into a chair.

"That what?" I asked.

"Why don't *you* finish it?" he said.

"That you've been constantly unfaithful," I said.

I half expected him to leap out of the shadows. I tensed myself for it.

When he chuckled, my body jerked with the unexpected reaction.

"Unfaithful," he said.

"Is that all you have to say?" I asked.

I heard him stand abruptly, felt his baneful eyes on the back of my head. Then he walked around the couch and stood before the fireplace again. He clasped his hands in back of him.

"Unfaithful," he said. "Yes. And no."

"Is that supposed to be funny?" I asked.

"If you wish."

"See here, Richard!" I flared. "This is no—"

"—no laughing matter," he cut in. "This is grim business. This is serious. This is bad. This is . . . laughable."

He chuckled and stood looking at me in amusement.

"You know," he said, "I believe I'll tell you."

"If there's any decency in—"

"Decency?" He snorted. "What a slapstick word." He turned away and leaned against the fireplace, resting his forehead against his arms. He looked into the flames for a long time in silence. He seemed to have forgotten me. I coughed. He stirred and shifted on his feet.

"You recall my last book?" he asked.

"What of it?"

"Do you recall the character of Alice?"

"What about her?" I said impatiently, certain that he was evading the issue.

"It is with Alice," he said, "that I've been, as you so quaintly put it, unfaithful."

"Very funny," I said.

He turned and looked at me coldly.

"I should have expected this from you," he said. "Why did I think for a moment that you could possibly understand?"

"Are you serious?" I asked.

He barked a scornful laugh. "You fool! Can't you see that?"

He turned away and took deep breaths. Then he spoke as though he were speaking to himself.

"Alice became so real," he said, "that Mary believed in her existence. As a person. An actual person. And this is my unfaithfulness."

He looked over his shoulder at me.

"But why do I even mention this to you?" he said. "Why should I dare hope to penetrate that skull of yours?"

"You're lying," I said. "I know my sister better than that."

"Do you?" he said.

"It's a *lie*."

"Oh, go home," he said.

"Listen—"

"Did you hear me!" he shouted.

I sat without moving. He stood glaring at me, hands twitching at his sides. Finally he turned away.

"If it's true," I said, "explain it."

"I told you," he said in a bored voice.

"I want the truth," I said. "Mary is losing her mind and I want to know why."

He didn't move. I couldn't tell whether he was listening or not.

"I know you," I went on. "You don't care about her. You never did. You've always expected her to live on scraps from you; well, that much she expected. She was prepared to share you with your work . . . and yourself."

I stood.

"But this isn't intangible," I said angrily. "This is outright and cruel. And I want to know about it."

He sighed, then spoke with that shifting of mood that made him so inexplicable. His voice was almost gentle.

"You *are* a child," he said. "Impossibly and irremediably a child."

"Are you going to *tell* me?"

He turned with a look of unconcern on his face.

"I'll tell you what," he said. "Why don't you ask Mary whom I've been consorting with?"

I looked at him.

"Go ahead," he said. "Are you afraid?"

"All right," I said. "I will."

At the door I paused, about to say something threatening. I was afraid to say it. I went out.

I was about to close the door when I heard his voice. At first I thought he was calling after me. I turned around.

He wasn't talking to me.

"She is five foot seven," he said. "Her hair is thick and golden. Her eyes are green jewels. They sparkle in the firelight. Her skin is white and clear.

"She is long and sleek. Tawny as a cat that stretches on the hearth rug and rakes its nails across it. Her teeth are sparkling white. Her—"

His voice broke off, and I knew that he'd seen the half-open door.

I turned. Mary was standing beside me, staring at the doorway.

"Let's go in," I said.

She didn't say anything. I put my arm around her and pushed open the door.

"No," she said.

"Please."

Richard watched us dispassionately as we walked to the couch. I turned on the lamp.

"And how are *you*, sweetheart?" Richard asked.

She lowered her eyes. I sat beside her and took her hand.

Richard turned his back to us and looked at the fire again.

"Well," he said, "what now?"

"We're going to get this matter thrashed out," I said.

Mary tried to get up, but I held her back.

"We have to settle this now," I told her.

"We have to settle this now," mocked Richard.

"Damn you!" I cried.

"David, don't," Mary said. "It never helps."

Richard turned around and looked at her with a laugh.

"You know that, don't you?" he said. "At least we've managed to teach you that much."

"Mary," I said, "who is Alice?"

She closed her eyes. "Ask my husband," she said.

"Why, surely," Richard said. "Alice is a character in my last novel."

"That's a lie," she said. I could barely hear her voice.

"Eh?" Richard said. "What's that? Speak up, my dear."

"She said it was a lie!" I cried.

He moved his gaze to me.

"Control yourself," he warned.

I started to get up, but he quickly stepped over and closed his hands upon my shoulders.

"Don't forget yourself," he said. "You're such a little fellow. It would be a pity to break your neck."

"Tell us the truth," I said.

He pulled away his hands and went back to the fireplace.

"The truth, the truth," he chanted, "why do people want the truth? It never pleases them."

He ran a hand through his hair. Then he blew out a tired breath.

"Listen," he said, as though making one last effort, "Mary is the victim of a delusion."

I glanced aside. Mary had raised her head and was looking at him.

"Try to understand," he said. "The girl Alice is a fictional character. When my wife started to see her, well—" He shrugged. "She saw only a phantom, a figment of—"

"Why are you lying?" Mary cried. "I saw her in this very room with you!"

It was no use.

"Come on," I said, "I'll take you upstairs."

"Please," she whispered.

As we were leaving, I noticed him turning off the lamp again.

"Good night!" he called. "Pleasant dreams!"

I took her upstairs and made sure that she locked the bedroom door from the inside.

When I returned to the study, Richard was stretched out on the couch. I turned on the lamp.

"Leave it off," he said.

"I want it on."

He threw himself on his side. "Oh, go home, will you? Get the hell out of here and leave me alone."

I went around to the front of the couch. He sat up.

"Did you hear what I said?" he threatened.

"I want the truth."

He jumped up, and his powerful hands closed on my arms. "I said go!" he yelled.

My face must have gone blank with fear. His face suddenly relaxed and he shoved me down on the couch.

"Oh, why bother?" he said, going back to the fireplace. "All right, I'll tell you everything. I'd like to see your face when you hear it."

He rested one arm on the fireplace mantel and turned to me.

"In my first book there was a character named Erick. I don't expect you remember him. He was my first good character. Out of words I built flesh and blood and living force."

A look of recollection crossed his face.

"Erick came in here one night while I was writing. He sat down where you're sitting. Right there. We talked. He spoke in the way I had made him speak. We had a hell of a time. We discussed all the other people in the book. After a while, some of them came in, too. The ones that I had realized well."

"You're lying," I said.

"Lying! You idiot! You wanted your damn truth, didn't you? Well, here it is! Are you too ignorant to understand it?"

He glared at me, trying to control his fury.

"It went on like that," he continued. "And then I'd think, 'I want them to return to their spectral homes.' And soon they started to make excuses, and before long I was alone again. Not sure I hadn't dreamed it all."

He turned and was silent for a long time. Then a quiet laugh rumbled in his chest.

"I wrote a second book," he said, "but I was too anxious. I didn't know my people. They never lived."

He turned to me with a look of elation on his face.

"Then I wrote my third book. And *Alice*. She breathed and she lived. I could see her and know her. I could sit and look at her beauty. I could drink in the fragrance of her hair, run my fingers through it, caress her long smooth limbs, kiss those warm, exciting—"

He caught himself and looked at me.

"Do you understand?" he said. "Can you possibly appreciate this?"

A look of childlike desire to make me understand filled his face.

"Can't you visualize it?" he said excitedly. "She was alive, David. *Alive!* Not just a character on a printed page. She was real. You could touch her."

"Then Mary saw—" I said.

"Yes. Mary saw. One night I summoned Alice. She was right here, unclothed, standing in the heat, painted over with flickering gold, an incensing, blood-pounding creature . . ."

He bared his teeth.

"And then *she* came, my precious wife. She saw Alice. She cried out and shut the door and ran to hide her head. I sent Alice away. I ran and caught Mary on the stairs. I brought her down and showed her there was no one. She didn't believe me, of course. She thought Alice had gone out through that window over there."

He laughed loudly.

"Even though it was snowing outside!" he said.

His laughter stopped.

"You're the first I've told," he said. "And I'm only telling you because I have to share the wonder of it. I'd never meant to speak of it. Why should the sorcerer give away his sorcery, the magician market his wand? These things are mine, all mine."

He told me to turn off the lamp. Without a word I reached back and turned it off.

"Yes, David," he said. "My wife saw Alice."

He threw back his head and laughed again.

"But not the others," he said.

"Others?" A feeling of unreality pressed in on me.

"Yes!" he said, "the others! Do you know what happened after Alice came alive? No, of course you don't."

He leaned forward.

"After I created Alice, everything I imagined came to life. There was no struggle. I imagined a cat sleeping before the fireplace, I'd close my eyes and, opening them, I'd see it there, its bushy coat warm and crackling, its nose pink from the heat.

"*Everything*, David! Everything I wanted. Oh, what people I filled this house with! I had madmen and harlots embracing in the hallways. I'd send Mary away and have my house bursting its seams with demons' revelry.

"I held ancient debauches in the front hall; had a torrent of red wine pouring down the stairway. I made altars and sacrificed voting maidens; the floorboards were soaked with their blood. I held shrieking, howling orgies that filled my house with masses of lust-mad people writhing like worms. Everything living—*living!*"

He paused and caught his breath.

"Sometimes I felt sad and dismal," he said. "I filled my house with ugly, sorrowful people, silent people. I walked among them patting the shoulder of a clay-dripping corpse, chatting idly with a ghoul."

"You're insane," I muttered.

It seemed to relax him. He closed his eyes and turned away.

"Oh, God," he said wearily, "why do people always say the things I expect? Why can't they be a little original?"

He turned at the sound of my standing.

"Where do you think you're going?" he asked.

"I'm taking Mary away," I said.

"Good," he said.

I stared at him. I couldn't believe it. "Is that all she means to you?" I asked.

"Make up your mind," he said.

I backed toward the door.

"Everything you've told me is a lie," I said. "There aren't any people. You imagined it all. There isn't anything but the ugliness you've brought into my sister's life."

I jumped back. He whirled and before I could get out he had rushed over to me and grabbed my wrists in a steel grip. He dragged me back to the couch and pushed me down on it.

"She's five foot seven," he hissed. "Her hair is thick and golden. Her eyes are green jewels. They sparkle in the firelight. Her skin is white and clear."

A feeling of revulsion crawled over me.

"She is wearing a blue dress," he said. "It has jewels on the right shoulder."

I tried to get up. He shoved me back and, reaching out one arm, grabbed me by the hair.

"She's holding a book," he snarled. "What was the name of the book you gave your mother? On her birthday long ago?"

I gaped at him. His fingers wrenched hair off my scalp. White pain flared.

"What's the name?" he demanded.

"*Green Roses*," I said.

He let go of me and I slumped on the couch.

"That's the book," he said, "that Alice will be holding when she comes in this room."

He faced the door.

"Alice," he said. "Come upstairs, Alice. One step at a time. Now open the kitchen door. That's fine. Don't trip. That's it. Walk across the floor. Never mind the lights. Push open the swinging door in the dining room."

I caught my breath.

I heard a woman's heels clicking on the dining room floor. I pushed up and scuffed backwards into the shadows. I bumped into a chair and stood there.

The heels came closer.

"Come right in here, Alice," Richard said. "Closer and closer and—"

The door flew open and the shadow of a woman streamed across the floor.

She came in, exactly as Richard had described her.

Holding a book in her right hand.

She put it on the table behind the couch and walked up to him. She slid her red-nailed hands over his shoulders and kissed him.

"I've missed you," she said in a lazy, sensuous voice.

"What have you been doing?" he asked.

She ran a finger slowly across his cheek, an amused laugh bubbling in her throat.

"But you already know, darling," she said.

He clutched her shoulders. A look of rage crossed his face. Then he pulled her against him and kissed her violently. I gaped at them like a spying boy.

Their lips parted, and one of her hands slid like a serpent

into his hair. Richard looked over her shoulder at me, a smile on the corners of his mouth.

"My dear," he said, "I'd like you to meet David."

"Why, of course," she said, without turning, as though she already knew I was there.

"That's him cowering in shadows," Richard said.

She turned and looked at me. "Do come out of the shadows, David," she said.

She reached over the couch and put on the lamp. I flinched and pushed back against the chair.

"Frightened?" Alice said.

"Bashful," Richard said.

I tried to speak. The words caught in my throat.

"Did you say something?" Alice asked.

"*Monster!*" I whispered.

A look of mild surprise crossed her face.

"Why, David," she said.

She turned to Richard and held out her arms to the side as though offering herself for inspection.

"Am I a monster, darling?" she asked.

Richard laughed and pulled her against him. He kissed her neck. "My beautiful gold-haired monster," he said.

She left his embrace and came to me. I cringed back. She reached out one hand, and I felt the warm palm on my cheek. I shivered.

She leaned toward me. I could smell her perfume. I made a sound of fright. Her warm breath touched me, and I drew back with a shudder. "*No,*" I said.

Richard laughed. "That's a new one. The first rebuff of your career."

Alice shrugged and walked away from me. "I must say he's not the friendliest person I've met." She gloated at Richard. "Like the Duke, for instance."

His smile disappeared

"Don't talk about him," he said.

"But darling," she said mockingly, "you created him. How can you hate your own creation?"

He grabbed one of her wrists and squeezed it until the color drained from her face. She made no outcry.

"Don't ever try to fool me," he gasped.

"We'll see," she said.

Then her face relaxed. She looked over her shoulder.

"Oh, David," she said, "I brought you a book."

I stumbled to the table, felt their eyes on me. I reached out and picked up the book.

Green Roses.

My fingers went dead. The book slipped from them and thudded on the rug. It opened with a flutter, and I saw the title page. I knew the words by heart, for I had written them.

To Mommy on her birthday. Love, David.

"True," I muttered.

"Of course," I heard him say.

I kept backing up until I felt a chair against my legs. I sank down and stared dumbly at them, watched him caress her. The room seemed to whirl about me.

"This is worth the hours of waiting," he was saying. "It makes the torture seem like a just penance."

"Torture?" she said in an amused tone.

He dug his fingers into the tresses of her hair. He drew her close, their lips almost touching.

"You don't know how much of me went into your creation," he said. "You're not just another woman to me. You're more than anyone in the world. Because you're a part of me."

I couldn't bear to listen any longer. I pushed up and stumbled for the door.

"Where are you going?" he asked.

"To get my sister," I said.

"No," he said.

I turned around. "But you said—"

"I've changed my mind," he told me.

"Where *is* she?" Alice asked.

He glanced at her. "Why do you want to know?"

"I want to go and talk to her."

"No," he said. "You can't."

He was looking at me and didn't notice the look of hate that flickered over her face.

"Sit down," he told me.

"No."

"Sit down," he repeated, "or I'll destroy your sister."

I stared at him. Then, without a word, I went back to the chair.

"I want to see her," Alice said.

He grasped her arm. "I said no," he said. "You do what I tell you."

"Always?" she asked.

"Or your life is ended!" he cried.

He released her.

"Now you must go," he said. "You'll kiss me once and go back to your secret place. Until I want you again."

An emotionless smile raised her red lips. Then she leaned forward and kissed him.

"Goodbye," she said.

He pulled her close and looked into her eyes.

"Remember," he said. "As I say."

"Goodbye."

She moved away from him and I heard the door closed behind her. The sound of her heels faded.

Richard turned back to the fireplace.

He stayed that way. Slowly a hope that I could escape grew in me. I started to take off my shoes. If I could only get to the door without him seeing me . . . I stood.

My eyes never left him. His body seemed to waver in the firelight. I stepped slowly across the rug. One foot after another.

My hand was on the doorknob.

"A ten-foot cobra is climbing up my bedroom door," Richard said. "It is going to kill my wife."

I stared at him.

He hadn't even turned around.

I ran to him and clutched his arm. "Richard!"

Suddenly, from upstairs, a scream pierced the air.

Richard's head jerked around. A look of horror filled his face.

"No," he said.

He tore from my hold and rushed to the door. He flung it open and ran across the hall. I heard him cry out:

"It is gone! It has disappeared!"

I ran after him up the stairs.

I found him kneeling over her.

It was Alice—dead. Her cheeks were puffed, her eyes wide and staring. Under her right eye were two red punctures.

Richard was looking at her in disbelief. He reached down and touched her face with trembling fingers, felt for her heartbeat.

I looked at Alice's feet. She had taken off her shoes so Richard would not hear her on the stairs.

He picked her up, his face a blank. He started down the stairs and took her into the study.

I turned quickly.

Mary was standing in the bedroom doorway, looking down at the study.

I grabbed her hand. "We've got to go!" I said.

She didn't speak as I half dragged her down the long stairway and out the front door. I put her in my car.

"Drive to the highway and wait for me."

"But—"

"Don't argue," I said. She stared at me for a moment:

Then she turned and drove down the path. I watched the car roll onto the road. I turned and ran back into the house.

I found him kneeling beside the couch on which he had placed Alice's body.

He was holding her hand and stroking it. All the arrogance was gone. He looked as though he thought she was going to wake up in a moment.

I went over to him and put my hand on his shoulder. His head snapped back and he looked up at me.

"You've got to get rid of her," I said.

"The house is burning," he said.

The suddenness made me jump backwards. The walls had burst into flame. The drapes began to curl, the room abruptly thick with smoke.

"Richard!" I cried. "Stop it!"

He didn't answer. He only stared at Alice's puffed, white face and stroked her hand.

I knew it was hopeless. I rushed for the door. Just before I reached it, a sheet of flame blocked the way.

I whirled and looked at him.

He didn't want me to leave.

I coughed as the choking fumes entered my throat. Turning, I ran for the window. Flames covered it.

I jerked a small table from the floor and hurled it at the window. It splintered through. I dived for the opening.

"No!" I heard him yell. It made me jolt to a halt.

"You *can't go!*" he cried. His words broke off into a peal of laughter.

"You can't stop me!" I cried.

He didn't say anything, just smiled and sank across her body.

Suddenly I knew why I couldn't go.

Because I'm one of his characters, too.

And now I'm waiting.

The Last Blah in the Etc.

You are awake, pale thing, your muddy eyes perusing.
There the ceiling, there the walls; security in plaster and
paint, in parchment jiggled with coordinate lilies. Primo:
goddam wallpaper. It is, has been and never more will be your
opening reflection. Secundo: *Mildred isajerk*. This thought
may continue.

Slumber-fogged, your gaze seeks out the clock. It has
not clarioned the dawn. It is, indeed, not even cognizant of
dawn's most rosy rise, its black arms pointing frozenly to
midnight's XII—

—or *noon!* You start, eyes bugged and marbleized, mouth
a precipitate sanctuary for some indigent gnat. *Wotnth'ell!*
And—*snap!* Body parallel with mattress becomes body
squared. You are—presto!—ninety degrees of male Ameri-
can athrob; a sitting inflammation. With a crunch of the
cervix, a crackle of the clavicle, you look around the room,
you look around the—

Silence. All and only silence. (Pallid thing)

"Mil!" you call. What, no sibilance of frizzling bacon, no
scent of coffee? "Millie!" No savor of charred toast, no lilt of
nagging on the air?

"Mildred!" *Wot'nth'blublazinghellis*—

Silence. Oh so silent.

Your brow is rill-eroded now. A curious dismay guerrillas
in your craw. Too silent this. Too—*deadly silent*. Yes?

"MILDRED!"

Ah, no reply, blanched thing. Your corn-cobbed toes
compress the rug, your torso goes aloft, you find erection.
"What's goin' on?" mumble you. You thump across the

room, shanks athwart, terror tapping tunes along your spine. You reach the hall. "Mil!" you cry. No Mil. The hallway is your racetrack. You are Mercury and Ariel. You are Puck in pink pajamas. "Millie!" No Millie. You blunder like a village-razing mammoth through the chambers of your home. "Mildred!"

No—need I append?—Mildred.

In fact, nothing. Whether sign of exodus, Goinghometo-mother note or hint of counternatural removal. Pale thing, you are aghast. Panic rings the tocsin in your wooly brain. Where—eh?—is Mildred? Why—ask you—at noon, are you alone, self-wakened?

Noon? But see, the black arms still point alike.

The clock has stopped.

Pulsing with alarm, you seek the phone, *le pachyderme en difficulté*. Digits clutch receiver, receiver cups ear. Hark; you listen. Your mouth is cavernized anew. Why?

Dead as the doornail, (proverbial) That's why.

"Hello," you state, regardless. You tap distress rhythms. "Hello! Hello! *Hey!*"

No answer. (Achromatic you)You drop the dumb Bell and worry a channel to the windows. You yank the cord and up goes the shade, flapping in maniacal orbits around its roller and through this paneful frame you view the picture of your street.

Empty.

"Huh?" Your very word. *"Wot the—"*

Strange tides rise darkly. Terror is a blankness. It is cessation, emptiness; figures, fog-licked, hardly heard, vaguely seen. "Mil?" you mutter.

No Mil.

Dress! Probe! Nose out! Get to bottom! Resolution hammers manly nails; your framework bolsters. Up—you vow —and at them. There's an explanation for everything. (Of course) You are the captain of your shape, the master of your soles. Once more into the britches! Onward!

Etiolated thing.

Bones garbed *vitement*, feet ensconced in Thom McCann's, you plunge through bedroom, hall, living room, kitchen, out through doorway and—

The neighbors! *The crossthehallwhydon'ttheymindtheirown-dambusiness* neighbors!

You arc the gap to their door, heartbeat a cardiac ragtime. Manifest really. (Sez you to you) Mil, Millie, Mildred, MIL-DRED has gone to pirate a dole of flour, a driblet of sugar. She laughs, blabbing and blabs, laughing with the neighbor's wife. She forgets old mortality. (Oohwilugiverhell!) And the phone lines suffer breach. *Q:* And the barren street? *A:* Nearby, a parade, a fire, an accident alluringly sanguineous and the neighborhood emptying to view it.

Only this and nothing more. (Rationalize chalky, poem-lifting you)

Forthwith: Skin-puffed knuckles harden, your hand is become a fist. Rap, rap, it goes. Inside, silence. Knock, knock. Ditto. Bang, bang. Also. You bluff. "Hullo!" you call, "Anyone t'home?"

No reply. *Boom!* You teach the door a lesson. But nothing. Terror-veined fury claims you. You twist the knob, the door creaks open.

Consternation.

No Mildred, no neighbors. The kitchen devoid of all —save (shade of *Marie-Celeste?*) a skilletful of orange-eyed eyes, awash in sibilant butter; a flame-perched pot with a delicate volcano of coffee in its dome; a toaster ticking like a chrome-cased bomb; the table set.

"*Hey.*" The cry drips feebly from your lips. "Where *is* everybody?" (Where, indeed?) You clump into the living room. Devoid. The bedrooms, all—bodiless. Your next remark, wan thing? I quote.

"What's goin' *on* here?" (*Un*—as you say—*quote*)

Now resolution finger-dangles from the sawed-edge cliff of fear. (*Quelle* tasty simile) Standing at the window, heart an eighty-mile-an-hour piston, you gape down at the street again. Empty; so empty. Panic looms.

"No!" Underground resistance again. Chin up, gauntlet down. *Avant!* Socratic you will plumb this poser to its roots. This Too Shall Pass!

You betcha.

Whirling, you greyhound to the door and exit. Pegasus could not pass you on the stairs—or make more noise. Three flights cannon-balling and the vestibule is yours.

Confusion plus. Boxes bulging mail like any day. Delivered papers strewn as always. "Huh?" Your quasi-gibbous eyes peruse the headline. *FIND STARLET TORSO IN FIRKIN.* No answer there. You plunge into the street, exploring.

One vast length of nothing, sir. One spacious, sidewalk-sided span of silence. (*Quelle* alliteration) In the middle of the street you stand, goggling. *Ovez*—nothing. Not one soul, one movement. You are alone—blank, marmoreal thing.

"*No!*" cries the hero—that's you. You slam the door in evidence's face. This cannot be! There Has To Be A Reasonable Explanation. Things Like This Just Don't Happen. (It says where?) Terror ricochets off reason's wall and comes back courage. You're off!

Ah, picture you, sallow, slapdash sleuth you are, running a forty-minute mile to Main Street, pulpy legs awaggle, breath like radiator steam; The Picture Of Durance in Grey. Along the crypt-still thoroughfare you scud, hunting for a fellow soul.

Doorbell ringing is futility you've found; knocking, a bootless cause; peering in at windows, inutility at its primest. Worse than inutility—*guignol* with its actorless scenes of a.m. enterprise—food boiling, frying, toasting, poaching;

tables set and stoves alive. And even, propped on sugar bowls, the morning papers.

But no one there to eat, serve, read.

Onward. (Every Effect Has Its Cause) (*Naturellement*)

Approaching Main Street you come upon a fresh obscurity. A halted car standing in its proper lane, hood still pulsing with engine tremors. Standing there as though its operator were waiting for the lights to change.

Empty though. (Ice mice batten on your heart) You waver beside its open window, staring in. A bag of groceries sags beside the driver's place; a morning paper next to that. *BUTT HOLDS STARLET*, reads the head. No aid there.

"I don't *get* it," you announce. (You will, discolored thing) Painpoints etch lines around your face. Your fingers tremble, your glands secrete.

Courage, mon passé.

You press on again, then, apace, return to take the car. Desperate dilemmas dictate desperate deeds. (*Quelle* something or other) Sliding in behind the wheel, you slap the gears into mesh (The hand brake isn't even out) and press the pedal mightily. The car leaps off with gas-fed growlings. The silence is undone.

A thought! Hunching forward, you finger prod a silvery radio button, then, leaning back, await.

A moment.

", *lo*-ve," sings a woman, "*lo*-ve, *lo*-ve," in eerie oscillating weariness, "*lo*-ve, *lo*-ve, *lo*-ve,"

Somewhere, a diamond needle, groove-imprisoned, pendulums the word, untouched because unheard. A city station too. Does that mean the city is tenantless? What about—

—the world? Yes, that too, (To you) dun, albescent, pale as witches thing.

", *lo*-ve, *lo*-ve, *lo*-ve, *lo*-" You cut her off, poking in another button. Silence. Another button. Ditto. Another, the same.

Another. ", *lo*-ve, *lo*-ve, *lo*-ve," You're back again. Eyes frozen grapes, you snap the radio off. Nothing but nerve impalings there.

Drive on. Drive on. Drive on and on.

Main Street's intersection. You signal for a turn, abash, draw in your arm. You turn—

—and, horror-tossed, slam on the brakes, stalling the motor. Breath hisses in and chills.

"*Gudgawd!*" (Literal translation)

'Til now there was a chamber in your brain that still housed disbelief. A chamber of contention with the facts. *Q:* So what was it? *A:* Everyone in town, by some strange rule of mob, was gone to view a movie star, the President, a fire, an accident, some incredible attraction. That was why the streets were empty, the houses *extempore* exited.

But no. The length of Main Street is a humanless alley strewn with unmoving, engine-purring cars. You stare at this, candescence. You gape upon a people-reft world. You are struck dumb with cognizance.

"No," you mutter. (Yes) "Oh, no." (Oh, yes) "*No!*" (Ah, but yes)

Oozing, mindless, from the car, you stumble forth, stricken as a zombie. Legged on wooden struts you clump across the gutter, goggle-eyed. No, you insist, despite the obvious; No, it can't be true. Denial breeds traction though. And gestation nears completion. In cob-webbed wombs stirs lunacy.

"Hey!" you howl, "*Hey-ey!*"

Snarling, you leap the curb and elephant your way along the sidewalk.

First National Bank. You fling your jangled self into the pie-slice opening of its revolving door and, spinning a desperate arc, plunge inside. Yelling. "*Hey-ey!* HEY!"

Silence.

"HEY-EY!"

The aberration of your voice handballs off marble walls, ricochets from polished v.p. desk and wriggles, troublous, between the bars of empty teller cages.

Unnerving you. Whirling, hissing, shaking, you exit *à pas de géant* (Running like hell) too distraught to concentrate on stealing money.

The street again. You rush into a woman's shop, clods thumping on the rug. You race by rows of dress racks.

"Hey!" you call, "Anyone here!" No one. You exit.

An appliance store—row on row of stoves and sinks and washing machines—snowy headstones in a linoleum churchyard.

"Hello!" you shout, "Hel-*LO!*" No reply. (You'll crack soon)

Turning, you find the street again, ice cubes dancing in your stomach. A candy store. You dash against its newsstand and headlines leap at you. *STARLET WEDGED IN CRUSE; TORSO OF ACTRESS FOUND IN TUN; STARLET BODY IN DEMIJOHN.* And, on one, in tiny letters, near the bottom. *Strange Sighting.*

(Ain't it the way?—wan, wishy-washy thing?)

Where was I?

Oh. You tear your gaze away and stare into the candy store. Empty; silent. Cups and dishes strew the counter, unattended. And *hark:* behind the counter, a malted mixer buzzes like an outboard motor in the distance.

"No," you mutter. (Thirty-forty seconds at the outside) "No. Hello! *Dammit, Hel-LOOOOO!*" Fury adds its rabid spine to fear.

They can't do this to *you!*

"*HEY-EY-EY-EY!*"

You stagger-swoop along the middle of Main Street, bypassing cars like raging tide around islands. "*HEY-EY!*" You cry havoc. "WHERE'N'TH'HELL *IS* EVERYBODY!"

Breath gives out. A stitch (in time) pokes needlepoints

into your side. Pupils like worlds swimming in chaos, your eyes whip around, searching. There has to be *an answer*. Your head yaws back and forth. *There has to be an answer.* Fury rises. *There has to be AN ANSWER!*

"There *has* to be!" you scream.

And, sired by malfunction, rage is born. (Right on schedule)

Hell-fire-eyed, you rush into a pottery shop.

"HEL-*LO!*" you challenge. No reply. Your lips compress.

"I said HEL-*LO!*" you ultimatum.

No reply.

Pulsing with distemper, you grab a firkin mug and let fly. Strike one! A hand-wrought chafing dish explodes into china shrapnel. The floor is sprinkled with its splinters. Angry satisfaction fires your insides.

"*Well?*" you ask. Nothing.

Your hand shoots out and grabs a miniature patella. *Whiz-z-z-z!*—it goes. Ca-*rash!* Strike two! A hail of gold-fringed porringer fragments sprays the floor and wall.

"I SAID HELLO!" you shout. Not mad exactly; more infuriated than deranged. Arm extended, spar-like, you pound along the counter, sweeping trenchers, salvers, goblets, bowls and cylixs into one great Dresden bomb.

Which goes off with a glorious, ceramic detonation, pelting kaleidoscopic teeth just everywhere. *Strike three!* You are fulfilled.

"There!" you yell.

Whirling, profanations dancing on your tongue, you rush from the shop, laughing. (A laugh not wholly wholesome)

"HEY!" you cry, "HEY-EY!" You shuck out curses at the people-less stretch of Main Street. You jump into a running car and drive along the sidewalk for a block, making a right turn into the window of a furniture store.

"Look *out!*" You bound into the ruins and begin to topple chairs and sling sofa cushions at the chandeliers. "I said Hel-

LO!" You kick in coffee table tops. You pick up porcelain lamps and pitch them at the walls. "HEL-L-*O!*"

And so on—hoary thing.

When next seen, hours later, you have run amuck, an abstract lamp shade for a hat, an ermine wrap around your camel's hair clad shoulders. You have burst into a supermarket with an axe and chopped pies and breads and cookies into flotsam. You have sent thirty cars running toward the neighboring town. You have thrown fistfuls of hundred dollar bills off roofs. You have set fire to the fire department, then driven its ladder truck on Main Street, knocking over hydrants and lampposts, leaving it, finally, red and running, in the lobby of the Gaiety Theatre.

And now you sit, wearied with rage's labor, sprawled on a contour chair you've dragged into the street; watching your town go up in smoke. Thinking: Who cares, gawdammit, anyway, *who cares?*

Which is—precisely, may I say?—the way we planned it.

For there is, of course, an answer. (As you said) An Explanation For Everything. A Cause For Every Effect. (As you also said)

We beamed down the brain waves at midnight, putting every child and woman into a semi-permanent coma. Making every man a solipsist.

Picture it. A world of men, each one believing himself to be the only one. Panic, madness, fury—all releasing the instincts (or habits?) of destruction. Making it so easy for us to complete our costless and wholly entertaining invasion.

Of course a good many men just stayed in bed and smiled indulgently. Men like you made up for that—you ghastly, hueless, biped, two-eyed *thing*.

Phone Call from Across the Street

HULLO?
Is that you, Joe?

Yeah, yeah, this is Joe. Who's calling me?

This is a friend of yours Joe. A good friend. How are you doing?

Who is this?

How are you doing Joe? I hear they got you pinned down Joe.

Yeah! Nobody got *me* pinned down. I got plenty ammo. Nobody's gonna get *me*.

How do you know, Joe? You're surrounded.

Yeah, that's what you, say who is this? A copper?

No, no, Joe. I told you. I'm your friend.

Yeah, well I got no friend in town.

Sure you have, Joe. You have me. So you're doing all right, haah Joe?

Who is this?

That's the stuff Joe. Don't you give up now. You just keep shooting, hear? Shoot a few for me, Joe.

Who is this, I said. I ain't got no time for talking.

No, you haven't got much time for talking, have you? You better go on over to the window and shoot some policemen Joe. Then you come back and talk to me. Will you do that Joe? Will you?

This ain't no copper?

No, Joe. Nobody hates the law more than me. Will you talk to me after you shoot some cops Joe?

Yeah, maybe. Yeah! Hang on. I got to go blast some coppers. Yeah, you hang on, I'll be back.

I won't go away Joe. No, I won't go away. Not me, Joe. I'll just sit here and look out my window. I'll just sit here and look across the street at you. Now I can see you Joe. You're at the window. I can hear your gun firing. *Bang, bang!* There it goes Joe. I can see you Joe. I can see your white face, all twisted. You're nuts Joe. Did you know that? Quiet and stolid and nutty as they come. Oh, *look.* You're laughing Joe. My my. *That's* the stuff. Laugh! Laugh like crazy Joe. It's all funny as hell and I mean it. You in your furnished room pinned down by the cops. That's funny. The cops firing their guns at you. You firing your gun at them. That's funny. It's all funny Joe. Especially death sitting on your shoulders Joe. That's a scream. *Again* Joe! Fire again. That's it. Empty your revolver. Make those bullets skip on the sidewalk and crunch holes in the cars and the buildings and the people. Ain't we got fun Joe? Boy, what fun! Show them who you are Joe! How few of us can. There goes Joe Vermilio, thief and murderer. Out like a spent rocket. Bango! That's the stuff Joe. Kill some more. *Kill them all!* I'd like that. That's my boy Joe. I'm proud of you. Keep it up. Keep it . . .

Hullo?

Well, hello there. That was very good Joe.

Huh?

Why, I can see you Joe. I'm watching you.

Where are you? Are you across the street?

That's right Joe. I'm across the street.

Can I see you? You can see me?

Sure, I can see you Joe. Of course I can. But you can't see me. Nobody can.

Yeah. Did you see that cop, hey? Did you see him run for it?

Sure Joe. I saw that. That was terrific. You were terrific Joe. You were sensational.

Yeah! Yeah, that's right. Say, who is this?

You show them Joe. You tell them who you are. You just

keep killing them and killing them. Yell at them Joe! Tell
them all what bastards they are.

Say who . . .

Tell them Joe!

Yeah! That's right. I'll tell them.

Go on Joe! Joe Vermilio. *The winner!*

They ain't getting *me.*

Of course not Joe. They'll never get you.

Hey, who is this?

I told you Joe. I'm your friend. I'm your best friend. I'm
your only friend in the whole world Joe. I called you up to
cheer you.

What's your name?

Don't stand there talking Joe. Go on and . . .

Uh!

What's the matter Joe?

Bastards! Got me in the arm. I'll get you for that, you bastards. I'll kill you all!

In the arm, eh? How does it feel Joe?

Ooooh, my arm. . . .

How does the hot lead feel Joe? Is it cooled off yet? Bleed-
ing? What does it look like Joe? Haah? Describe it.

Oooooh, God it hurts.

Well, you go right over to the window and shoot your gun
at them Joe. Who do they think they are anyway, wounding
you? I wouldn't take that Joe. I just wouldn't take it. I'd go
over to the window and scream at them. Get even with them
Joe. *Kill them!*

I'll kill you, you bastards!

I can hear you running over the rug Joe. Like the madman
that you are. Like the stupid puerile ox that you are. You're
caught Joe. You don't know it Joe but you're trapped like
a fish in a net. What a dope you are Joe. How stupid and
hopeless you are. You're pathetic Joe. Did you know that?
Pathetic, that's what you are. Ah, there you are. Your face is

so white Joe. Why didn't you ever go out in the sun? Oh well, there'll be heat enough soon Joe. Soon. Oh look! There's blood on your nice white shirt. How colorfully it stands out. Stunning, Joe. All shot up aren't you Joe? My my. I'll let you in on a secret Joe. The police are trying to kill you. Know that? But we won't let them get you will we Joe? Not us. We're big pals Joe. You're a big stupid ox but that doesn't matter. I can use you. Go on! Fire. Bang, bang, *bang!* One, two, three. Give it to them Joe. Kill them all!

I got one, I got one! You *see* it! I got one!

Why if it isn't my old friend Joe Vermilio.

I got one haah?

Does your arm hurt Joe?

Naah. I got one haah? I showed them didn't I?

You showed them Joe. You showed them all right.

They ain't going to get me are they?

Why, certainly not Joe Vermilio, my old friend. How could we allow that, Joe Vermilio, my very old friend.

Hey, this Mike Tucci?

Mike Tucci, Joe? He's dead. Didn't you know that Joe?

Mike Tucci? Mike Tucci is dead?

Sure, Joe. He's dead.

God, I didn't know that.

Don't call me that Joe. Yes, he's dead Joe. Like to talk about Mike Tucci, Joe? Like to . . .

They ain't getting me though, haah?

They won't get you Joe. You'll get away. Far away.

Hey, you got a car! You got a way haah?

A car Joe? No. I haven't got a car Joe. But a way? Sure, Joe, I got a million ways.

What do you . . . *aaaah!*

Joe? Joe, what's wrong, Joe? Can you hear me Joe? What's the matter?

I . . . I . . . can't . . . breathe. They . . . they shot . . . . *teargas!*

Oh, really? My goodness Joe. You should do something

for that cough. I guess there's nothing more you have to say Joseph Anthony Vermilio, thief and murderer. Joe? Joseph, can you hear me? Joe don't stop shooting. Don't stop just because you ... *There*. That's the stuff. Break the window. Get fresh air. Shoot them Joe. Oh, go back! They have machine guns. *Look out!*.....................Oh. Look at you Joe. Aren't you a sight. Holes all over you. For crying out loud Joe, haven't you any sense at all. Well that's what I call a ... well, would you look at that. There! That's my boy Joe! *Crawl* Joe! That's it. Hang on to the window sill with those *bloody* hands. Hang on Joe. Shoot them all Joe. That's the stuff...................Oh Jo-*oe*. Are you there Joe? All I can hear is teargas hissing. Well they're not firing anymore anyway Joe. Quiet isn't it? Joe? Can you hear me Joe? Where's your *spirit* Joe Vermilio? Come *on* now Joe. Don't let a few dozen slugs slow you down. Aw, come on. Don't quit on me Joe.................Oh, would you listen to that. They're chopping down your door Joe. Now are you going to stand for that Joe? What's the *matter* with you? Don't let them get away with that Joe ....Say, why don't you join me on the roof Joe? There's a gorgeous sunset. I can see it from here. Well, would you look at those pink clouds. Gorgeous, Joe. Just gorgeous. I ... what?

Who's this calling?

Oh, are you the police? Have you done away with Joe Vermilio?

Who *is* this?

Oh, you wouldn't know me officer. Not at the moment. Say now, incidentally, is Joe Vermilio dead?

Yeah, yeah, he's dead. Look, uh, hang on will you. I'd like to talk this over for a while. I ...

You want to trace the call? You're having some poor idiot try to trace the call. You want to find out who I am. That's pretty funny officer. Most people won't have anything to do with me. Come along officer. Even if I told you who I was,

you wouldn't believe me. I'll let you know. Later. Tell you
what though. If you're really anxious to know who I am, you
ask Joe Vermilio. He knows who I am. Ha ha ha ha ha. Don't
you Joe? You ask him. Go ahead. Ask him who I am................
Goodbye now.

Maybe You Remember Him

G OOD EVENING, SPORTS FANS. It's Wednesday night
again and Columbia brings you another look into
Yesterday's World of Sports. Look back with us to last year, to
the last decade, the last century. See the great fighters, the
football stars, the tennis champions, the baseball wonders of
yesteryear. All the immortals brought to life again in—*Yesterday's World of Sports*.

"And here to bring you tonight's story and introduce
tonight's guest is the noted sports columnist and commen-
tater—your host—Max Haney."

"Good evening friends. I think we have a story tonight
you'll be thinking about for a long time. Because it's a little
out of the ordinary, a step away from the usual sports story.
Oh yes, it's a tale of the avid young sports fan who grew up
to match and top the records of his former idols. But with
a difference. And, sure, it's the story of a young man who
wanted to be a sports star more than anything else in the
world. It's *that* story—but with a twist. A twist you might
not believe but one you won't forget.

"Maybe you remember him. His name was Harry Campbell. A little before your time? Well, maybe. Harry's pitching
days ended thirty-five years ago. But ask the old timers and
look at the records. Ask his old battery mate Jess Chandler—
the way we're going to ask him later in the program. They'll
tell you Harry was the greatest pitcher who ever lived and
then some. Why?

"Let's see why."

"Here we go into the ninth inning with Harry Campbell

still holding the Indian sign on the Cards. We're about to see baseball history made, ladies and gentlemen. If old Harry can finish this inning without giving up a run, if he can get just three more outs, he'll have his three hundredth win —*without a loss*. Just ten years ago Harry Campbell broke into baseball with the Brooklyn club and every year, like clockwork—thirty wins and no losses. Last week he won his twenty-ninth of this year and now he's three outs from his thirtieth.

"The infield is tossing the ball around. Now Harry has it, he's rubbing it up. The slightly built pitcher takes off his cap and wipes his brow. The crowd gives a cheer as Harry uncovers his bald head. It's an old game they play with Harry, kidding him about his forty-seven years. *Forty-seven*. At a time when other players are coaching from the line or the bench old Harry is firing that ball in like a nineteen-year-old rookie. And about to reach a baseball pinnacle.

"First batter is Johnny Dugan, Card second sacker. Johnny's dropped from .356 to .349 today with a trio of goose-eggs from Harry. Campbell pumps once, twice, here's the pitch. Strike one, nicking the inside corner. Johnny taps the plate once. Harry doesn't waste a minute, he goes right into the next motion.

"*Strike* two—nicking the inside corner again. Dugan tenses himself now. Harry shakes off one signal, another one. Now he nods, goes into the wind-up. Here it comes.

"Strike three!—and Johnny Dugan takes it looking. He drags his bat away without a squawk. That's Campbell's nineteenth strike-out of the game. They all look forlorn against old Harry. He handles the league leaders like he handles the bushers. There doesn't seem to be anybody who can touch him. Thirty wins a year *every single* year for ten years. Man, that's a record and Harry is only two outs away from it.

"Rip Hutson at the plate now, Rip standing in at a not too frightening .283 but with 94 runs batted in and 26 home runs. Rip bats from both sides of the plate. He's trying it lefty again. Doesn't seem to matter much to Harry which way they stand, he blows them over one way or the other. If we sound like we're raving, folks, forgive us but you just can't help raving about Harry. Here's a player who started when other players are about ready to quit—and then proceeded to rack up the most sensational pitching record in the history of the game—299 wins against no losses, 3120 strikeouts and . . . here's the pitch.

"Strike one, if that's any surprise. Right down the groove. Harry seems to have every batter on mental file, knows just where their weaknesses are. There's that familiar pumping motion, once, twice, the kick the three-quarter over-arm delivery, the wrist snap and there's the pitch. Hutson takes a cut and tops the ball. It rolls straight at Campbell. Harry picks it up, tosses to Serena at first. Hutson out by five steps.

"One more out now and Mr. Harry Campbell of Bay Shore, Long Island hits top pedestal in the baseball hall of fame. He's there already, of course, fifty times over. That's how many perfect games he's pitched. *Fifty* of them—count them—fifty no-hit, no-run games. And no-walk games. I think Harry's walked about fifty men in his whole career. What was it Mark Fowler of the Pirates said about Harry Campbell last season?—*The guy ain't human.*

"I'm almost inclined to agree with him.

"Last batter, Mickey Atwell. The fans are leaning forward in their seats now. There's hardly a sound in the ball park. Atwell swinging two clubs. He tosses one away. You can hear the sound of it hitting the ground. Old Harry waiting grimly, hasn't cracked a smile all day. He's been that way all season too. Used to be when he first started, Harry was all smiles and . . .

"Here's the motion, kick, delivery—*Strike* one. Chandler fires the ball back. Campbell takes off his glove and rubs the ball. Now he steps back on the mound. Shakes his head . . . nods. Sets himself. Here's the pitch.

"Ball one—high outside. You can almost hear the people catch their breath. Everyone is riding on those pitches now. They want to see old Harry in the Hall of Fame.

"Another pitch. Atwell swings—he gets a hold of it! The ball is rising fast heading down the left field line. There's no doubt where it's going but is it or isn't it . . .

"Foul! Just by a whisker. The stands rumble with excitement. Old Harry just standing out there steady as a rock. What *nerves*. He gets a new ball, he's rubbing it up. That was strike two, count of one and two now against Atwell.

"Now Harry is ready. He's standing there and looking at the plate. He doesn't move a muscle. Now he steps on the mound. He almost steps back but then he catches himself! A close one, he almost balked. Now he looks for the signal. He nods. He stands there with his arms hanging at his sides. No motion yet, he just stands there looking straight ahead. I wonder if anything's wrong.

"Nothing apparently. Now he winds-up once, twice, sets himself and . . .

"Harry Campbell sits with the baseball gods!"

"That was a recording you just heard—made the day Harry Campbell won his three hundredth game without a loss and his seventy-fifth shutout and . . . maybe you see why they call him the greatest pitcher who ever lived. Three hundred wins and no losses. Fifty perfect no-hit, no run, no-walk games. Seventy five shut-outs. Three thousand, one hundred and twenty two strike-outs. And a total earned run average of 1.32 for ten years. No wonder Mark Fowler said what he did that day so long ago. I'm inclined to agree with him too.

"And therein lies our real story. Unbelievable, yes, but Jess Chandler swears it's true and who can deny what happened that first day of the 1976 World Series. It's in the books.

"Our guest—one of baseball's great receivers—Jess Chandler. How are you Jess?"

"Pretty well, thank you, Mr. Haney."

"I'd like you to tell our listeners your story, Jess."

"I'd be glad to, Mr. Haney."

"Ladies and gentlemen—the story behind that ill-fated afternoon, the story of what happened to Harry Campbell."

I kept watching Harry that afternoon when they carried him off the field. He had a smile but it was frozen on, like he felt he owed it to the people. And I remembered something he said once to me. He said even a man on the scaffold can smile.

I moved down the long tunnel while they carried Harry to the showers. The boys weren't only yelling for Harry. We had a World Series coming up too, our first in five years. Even a thirty-game winner can't pitch you into the Series all by himself.

And, somehow, no offense meant, Harry never seemed to really do us any good. That's not as crazy as it sounds. Sure he won thirty games every year of his ten years with us—but they were always his first thirty. What I mean is he always won his first thirty starts—no matter who he pitched against. And then, right after his thirtieth—*he was through for the season*.

We never knew why. He didn't quit or anything but he might as well have. He seemed to be pitching in a vacuum all by himself. After his thirtieth win something always came up. One year he'd pull an arm muscle and have to sit it out the rest of the season. Another year his mother got sick and Harry had to take care of her. Then, maybe another year, he'd pitch—and get knocked out of the box in the first or second inning. It was crazy. He never got tagged with a loss but still he got knocked out. It got so we all kidded about it around the fourth year Harry was with us. Every time he'd win his thirtieth game we'd all say—*well . . . that's that*.

Another thing. Harry was never a team man. It didn't really seem to matter to him if he was pitching in an important series or against the cellar team. It didn't seem to matter to him that he had a team behind him. He was out for his thirty wins and he got them and that was all for the year. Now, honestly, I'm not knocking Harry. What I've just said has been written about a thousand times in articles and books. Harry was a nice, quiet guy but . . .

As I said though, this tenth year our manager decided to play it cagey. Why he never thought of it before I don't know but he didn't. I mean pitching Harry every fifth game or so, so that Harry didn't get his thirtieth until September and he was still in good shape. We were banking on him coming through in the Series and giving us our first championship.

Harry wasn't happy that day—that was easy to see. Three hundred wins and he sat on the locker room bench like a condemned prisoner. Every one kept slapping him on the back and shaking his hand and he tried to smile but it just didn't come off. And it wasn't just *that* day.

I roomed with Harry and he'd been under the weather for close to a year. I mean really bad. He'd always been nervous, had the jumps but this last year it was getting terrible. I gave up counting the nights Harry used to toss on his bed groaning and the sweat pouring off him while he muttered things to himself I couldn't make out.

I'd seen some of that same sweat on him when Atwell poled that ball out of the park—foul. And all during the game too. But not because he was afraid he was going to lose it. He knew he'd win—he told me so before the game started. No that wasn't it.

He was afraid he was going to win it.

Anyway I went over to the bench and sat down beside Harry. I noticed him jump a little when I did.

"You better get out of those shorts, pop," I told him and I

saw his hands—the hands of a three hundred game winner:
They looked as if they couldn't even *hold* a baseball.

"I didn't see you," he said.

"What's wrong, Harry?" I asked him. "You should be in
the showers singing victory songs. You look sick."

"I'm all right," he said.

I patted him on the shoulder.

"You should be, you old dog," I said. "You're an immortal
now."

He stared at his hands for a second, then he exhaled slowly.

"Immortal," he said and something like a sob caught in
his throat.

"You sure nothing's wrong?" I asked.

He shook his head and I let it go. I figured if I'd just won
my three hundredth I'd be a little rocky too.

"I didn't even mind you nixing all my signals today," I told
him. "Man you were *really* loose today. You looked as if you
were trying to throw those pitches into the stands—and
every one of them came right in there."

His lips pressed together for a second.

"I was," he said, "I *was* trying to throw them into the
stands." He shivered. "But I couldn't do it," he said.

"What are you talking about?"

"Nothing, nothing," he said hurriedly, forcing a quick
unpleasant smile to his face. "I'm just kidding around, Jess."

I looked at his lean, sweat-streaked face, his thin black hair
surrounding the white bald spot. I punched him on the arm
lightly.

"Go on, get in the shower," I ordered him.

Later I sat and watched Harry dress and I kept thinking
about his pitching—about the way he always pitched his
own game never taking my advice or my signals more than
once or twice a game and even that more to please me than
anything else I think. I thought about how his delivery got
wilder and wilder every year without his accuracy changing

a bit. And I thought about what he'd told me before—how he tried to throw the ball into the stands and couldn't. He wasn't ribbing me. And when he said he *couldn't* I don't think he was talking about principles.

When he was putting on his hat and coat I went over and told him about the dinner the team was holding over in the Village that night. As manager of the party I invited him as our guest of honor.

"I can't make it, Jess," he said, "I'm sorry. I got business."

"*What?* Oh you're kidding, not *tonight!*"

"Tonight," he said.

And the way he said it gave me a chill. We were walking under the stands by then and I thought it was the dampness. Now I know what it was and the dampness had nothing to do with it.

"Can't you get out of it, Harry?" I asked.

He shook his head.

"I . . . I'd like to Jess but I can't. I can't get out of it."

His voice sounded hollow and lost and I found myself watching him as we trudged along heading for the exit. Every time we passed under an opening in the stands I saw the light move across his white face. Never tanned, Harry didn't. A whole season in the sun and he was still white.

There was a mob waiting at the gate for Harry. They were yelling and shoving and waving their autograph books. Harry sort of drew back when he saw them out there. His face was like a mask.

"Face it, pop," I said. "Face it. You're the greatest now."

"Oh, God," he said.

I never saw him look so bad as that late afternoon when he went out there to sign autographs. There was a twitch in his right cheek and when someone knocked off his hat and they all laughed and cheered at his bald head I saw his lips pull back from his teeth as if he was going to scream. He kept getting shoved and mauled while they pushed book after book under his face. I finally rescued him and half led him across the street to the garage where I kept my car. The mob followed us every inch of the way and they didn't back off until I almost ran down a few of them. Then they retreated, booing and hissing. At me, of course.

Harry didn't say anything while I headed for my place in the city. I was hoping I could talk him into going to the party that night. I didn't say anything either. Not until we were waiting out a light at the foot of Manhattan Bridge.

"You're gonna cancel your business engagement," I told him. "You're coming to our party. You need some relaxation, Harry, that's what you need."

He didn't seem to be listening to me but he shook his head once, his chin practically on his chest.

"No, Jess, no," he said. "I have to go."

"What's so important it can't wait till tomorrow?"

He just shook his head and shut up. I didn't say anymore until we reached my place and he came in for a drink. He said he could because his appointment wasn't until eight.

"Where are you going?" I asked him, handing him his drink.

"Out on the Island."

"Where, Bay Shore?"

"Around there."

"How you gonna get there, Harry?"

"I'll . . . take the Long Island Railroad, I guess."

"Well look," I said, "Take my car and . . ."

He shook his head.

"Why not?" I asked. "Take it. Maybe you can get back in time for some of the party."

"No," he said.

"Oh, for . . . !" I almost blew up but then I shrugged. "Well, take the car anyway," I said. "You can bring it back in the morning."

"I better not," he said, "Thanks anyway Jess. I . . ."

I put down my drink.

"Harry, for God's sake, what's *wrong?*" I asked him.

He seemed about to say something, then he stopped. He put down his drink as if he were going. Then he picked it up again and sank back on the couch cushions.

"I . . ." he started and gritted his teeth. "Jess, I don't want to get you mixed up in this."

"Harry, where are you going tonight?"

I saw his throat move. He looked like a hundred year old man sitting there. He stared into his drink with haunted eyes.

"I have to make a payment," he said.

"What . . . kind of payment Harry?"

He sat there a long time without looking at me. He stared into his glass and jiggled the ice cubes slowly. There was a battle going on in him, I could see that. As if he knew he had something terrible to tell and wanted to tell it but was afraid to involve me. I saw a line of sweat on his upper lip.

Then, abruptly, he put down his glass and pulled out his wallet. He fumbled nervously with it and finally drew out a small creased square of paper. He handed it to me and his hand shook helplessly.

"There," he said, "T—*there.*"

I opened up the paper and looked at it a long time before I understood. And then my stomach pulled in and my breath was gone.

"I.O.U.," it read, *"my soul."*

I looked up at him, the paper still in my fingers.

"I don't get it Harry," I said.

"That's what I'm paying tonight," he said and he put down his drink because his hand shook too much.

For a long time we sat there staring at each other. Outside we could hear cars passing in the street and upstairs I heard a woman laughing. This was New York, 1976, and everything was just as it had always been. Yet here I was holding a slip of paper that read *I.O.U., my soul* and underneath those words was Harry's signature in red but not red ink.

I looked up again from the slip.

"Tonight?" I said.

He looked at me bleakly. "That was the agreement," he said.

"When . . . when did this happen, Harry?"

I saw his throat move.

"I was thirty-six," he said.

Harry Campbell was drunk and he meant to get drunker and he was going to stay drunk. What else could a man do when he was thirty-six and a failure. He'd been married but that was ended. Virg had divorced him when he'd tried to clutch out and grab fleeting magic and only got a bar pickup and an adultery charge. Now he was alone and a failure. Virg was right even though she'd yelled it in bitterness and hate that night they'd separated. *You'll never get anywhere! You're useless, you'll end up in the gutter!*

She was right, that's where he'd end up.

He sat in the dark booth and stared ahead with sick eyes. A bitter chuckle sounded in his throat as he thought about his teens when he was the star pitcher for Bay Shore High. What a year, what a future; him with a record of 15 and 2 with 127 strike-outs. He'd been so certain of the future then. Oh, sure, the world was his oyster. What a laugh! Harry snickered and wanted to pick up his glass and fling it at the television set because it sat up there over the bar and reminded him. And mocked him.

This was all he had left. Odd jobs around town. Spending his spring afternoons and evenings in this bar, losing the summer days and nights here in this booth watching the ball games Brooklyn played. Trying to pretend he didn't notice the empathic twitch of degraded muscles in his arm that paralleled every pitch he watched. He just sat there dull eyed and ill and drank and watched ball games on the flickering screen.

Until that moment in that night when, in a fever of lost misery he had muttered through clenched teeth—*"I'd sell my soul to be pitching again."*

Then the man came into the bar.

It seemed nothing unusual. The man certainly was nothing unusual; just a moderately dressed man entering the bar on a July evening. He wore a plain summer suit and wore a woven hat with a colored hat band. He came over and sat down in the booth and asked Harry's pardon. All the bar stools were taken, he said and there were no empty booths and would Harry mind terribly?

Harry didn't notice the empty booth in back or the empty seat in the front of the bar. He just nodded gruffly and kept his glittering eyes on the television screen while in his tightly shut mouth his teeth remained clenched.

Then the man said, "So you'd like to pitch again."

Harry almost spilled his drink as his hand twitched violently on the smooth table top. He stared at the man blankly and felt a tremor in his stomach muscles.

"What?" he said.

"You'd like to pitch again," said the man.

Harry's throat moved and, almost instinctively, he pushed back against the wall of the booth. There was something in the man's eyes.

"How do you know?" he asked in a hollow voice.

The man chuckled. "Why, who doesn't remember your pitching exploits in high school? I've lived in Bay Shore a good many years. As a matter of fact I used to watch you pitch. You were destined for stardom. What happened?"

Harry's muscles unknotted. He didn't recognize the man but he recognized what the man was saying. What had happened? He'd married his school sweetheart that's what happened. She'd made him study law, that's what happened.

He'd enrolled at St. John's and flunked out and gotten a job as a Wall Street messenger and never gotten anywhere, that's what happened.

"That's too bad," said the man.

Again Harry jumped because the man seemed to be reading his thoughts.

"*What?*" It was all he could say.

"I was just thinking about your potential," the man said, "You could have made the major leagues with very little difficulty."

Harry grabbed at that straw because, after all, he was drowning.

"You . . . think so?" he said and he forgot the look in the man's eye because he liked what the man said.

"Very definitely," the man said. "You had every gift a top pitcher needs—control, a splendid eye, a good strong arm and the will to win. It was a shame you had to give it up."

"Yeah," Harry said, playing with his drink again. "A shame."

Be *practical*, Harry, he remembered. Pitching's a child's game. You can't make a decent *living* at it. You're good Harry but not good enough to make a decent living at it. Now *law* . . .

His thoughts trailed off and he suddenly picked up the glass and emptied it with one swallow.

"She was mistaken," was all the man said and then, before Harry could speak, the man pulled something from his inside vest pocket.

"My card," he said.

Harry stared at the man, then he picked up the card and read it.

Leonard De Ville, Manipulative Surgery

Harry blinked. "What's that?" he asked.

"Your passport to the major leagues," the man said.

★

Doctor De Ville's office was in a section of Bay Shore Harry had never been near—on the other side of the Long Island Railroad tracks. He walked slowly along the quiet, tree-lined street looking for the house number. The doctor had no downtown office. He told Harry that was because the Chamber of Commerce did not regard his profession as one entitled to the privilege of legality.

Harry really felt like a fool going to the man's office. He'd never in his life heard of *Manipulative Surgery*. Yet he was in no position to turn down any possible aid, he knew that. He was in just that state where he would grasp out at anything and this man had told him he could pitch again. *Him*, Harry Campbell, thirty-six, semi-balding, with a pot belly—promised the ability to pitch again. And not just in a local park with local amateurs. Pitching in the major leagues. It was insane but the man had said it and Harry knew he had to find out if it was true.

He found the place. There was no name outside but the house number was the one Doctor De Ville had scrawled on a scrap of paper. It was an old wooden house, vintage 1890 or thereabouts. Harry looked around as he went up the creaky porch steps. He didn't want anyone to see him, the doctor had said it was illegal.

The front door opened before he reached it and Doctor De Ville, in a white smock, met him and ushered him into a small, musty-smelling hall. It didn't smell like a doctor's office, Harry thought.

"Well, you see my brand of practice is not dependent on usual equipment," said the doctor.

Harry's head snapped around. There it was again, the man reading his mind.

"I could see from the look on your face that you doubted my profession," said Doctor De Ville. "Since my office does not resemble what you visualize as a doctor's office."

"Oh," said Harry.

They went right in and the doctor had Harry take off his suit coat and roll up his right shirt sleeve. He set Harry down on a leather-topped table in a room that was bare and dusty except for a desk and two chairs.

"My profession," said Doctor De Ville, "deals with the arrangement of musculature. We of Manipulative Surgery are of the opinion that it is in this skein of nerve, tendon, muscle, *et al.* that the physical abilities lie. It is, further, our contention, that no amount of time and abuse can change this ability so much that manipulative surgery cannot restore the old arrangement and, thus, the old abilities. To be brief," he said, seeing the blank look on Harry's face, "I massage your arm and when I am finished you will be as good a pitcher as ever you were. No, you will be even *better*. For that fine point of coordination you once possessed will be surpassed. You see the athlete possesses a muscular arrangement which is, purely through accident, the very compendium of mobile efficiencies. My profession," he concluded, "Takes these accidents of arrangements and reduces them to controllable actualities."

It sounded good to Harry. The doctor started to massage.

"I'm . . . not very well off," Harry said embarrassedly as the doctor rubbed and tapped, "I mean to get work but . . ."

"Say no more about it," said Doctor De Ville affably, "I'm glad to help you. Besides, well to be frank, we are mistrusted and there are not many who will allow us to work on them."

"I see," Harry said.

The office was quiet. There was no sound outside either. The sunlight filtered through the drawn shades and Harry watched the dust motes dancing in the sun as he lay there silently and felt the strong hands of the doctor on his arm. It might be true, what the doctor said. He did seem to feel a new strength in his arm, a rejuvenated ability.

"Of course," said the doctor, "There will be a slight payment. I am dependent to a point on my patients."

"Will it be more than . . . than I can afford?" Harry asked.

The doctor stopped working momentarily and looked Harry in the face.

"I don't think so," he said.

Then, very shortly, the massage was over and they sat at the desk and the doctor asked Harry if he had the slip of paper with the address on it. Harry took it out and gave it to the doctor. The doctor pulled out a fountain pen and, turning the slip of paper over, he wrote a few words on it. Then he slid the paper over to Harry.

"Payment," he said.

For a long time Harry stared at the paper without moving a muscle. Then he raised his eyes and looked into the bland eyes of Doctor De Ville.

"Is this a . . . *joke?*" he asked in a husky voice.

"A great joke," said the doctor. "Will you sign?"

Harry shuddered and shrank back against the chair.

"You may go," said the doctor, "without signing. However, as soon as you walk out the door your arm will be useless again. You'll never pitch."

The words made things simple. He sat there looking at the doctor.

"Then all this line about . . . manipul . . . that stuff. It was all just a lie to get me out here," he said.

"Not at all," said the doctor, "I merely neglected to tell you that no one on earth practices the profession but myself."

Harry felt his muscles growing tight.

"What if I sign?" he said.

The doctor raised his hands munificently.

"In that case," he said, "You can do anything you want in pitching."

Into Harry's mind crept the daydream he had so often comforted himself with during those periodic bouts of self pity. Him, a thirty game winner—no losses. Him with an endless string of wins, shut-outs, perfect games. The greatest pitcher who ever lived. Visions swallowed up the puny measurement of his soul.

So he leaned forward and, quickly, he signed the conditions of exchange.

"He got me a tryout with Montreal," Harry told me, still sitting there in my apartment. "No matter how I threw the ball I struck out the batter. I was a sensation. Next season I went to Brooklyn. You know the rest."

"And that was . . . ten years ago?" I said.

"Yes."

"Didn't you ever . . . try to get out of it?"

"My God," he said, his voice breaking, "I did everything I could, Jess. I went back to that house to tell him. He wasn't there, the house was empty." He drew in a shaking breath. "It was probably always empty."

He picked up his glass and stared into it.

"I tell you I tried *everything*. I tried balking but I couldn't get off the mound. I tried to throw the ball into the dirt but I couldn't, it'd rise up into the strike zone. I tried to heave it over your head into the stands and that was the season every sports writer was raving about my 'fabulous sinker.' "

"You never saw the . . . *doctor* again?" I asked.

"No," he said. "But I know he's waiting for me. Tonight I'm supposed to meet him at a roadhouse in North Bay Shore. And . . ."

He didn't finish, just sat there looking at me with stark, frightened eyes.

"Isn't there *anything* you can do, Harry?" I asked him.

"No," he said. "No, nothing. He said the conditions would be met in ten years and they were. I have to pay him tonight."

"Will you . . ." I started and could hardly finish, "*die?*"

He sat there motionlessly and looked at me.

"I don't know," he said.

Something shuddered down through me but I fought

it off. I got up and sat beside him. I put my arm around him.

"Listen pop," I said, *"Listen.* You're not going."

"I have to, Jess, I *have* to."

"Oh, there must be some way to get out of it. There has to be. He has no power over you."

"I signed a contract," he said.

"Contract," I said, "what contract? A lousy slip of paper with an address on the other side. Is that a contract you have do follow?"

"But I . . . signed it," Harry said. Then I saw something in his eyes, a sort of flicker. He put down the glass suddenly and stood up.

"Harry . . ."

"Wait a minute!" He silenced me. "I seem to remember, I seem to . . ."

It all welled into his face all of a sudden, hope and excitement.

"Yes!" he said, "An old common law that's never used anymore. But it's never been revoked. I remember reading it in a book once at St. John's."

He recited it slow as if he wanted to convince himself.

"Any contract written on paper which has irrelevant writing on the opposite side is not binding."

I started up.

"Harry, you got him!" I think I shouted and we wrung each other's hand and laughed and breathed again.

The first day of the 1976 World Series. Maybe you were there, sitting in the stands that day. Maybe you remember.

When I came into the locker room I found Harry there, already in his uniform, staring blankly at the metal door of his locker.

"Today's the day, pop!" I said.

He hardly budged, he didn't even look at me.

"Stop worrying," I told him. "It's in the bag."

Harry said, "I saw him."

I felt the tips of my fingers go numb.

"*Saw* him?"

"I was coming into the field," he said. "I looked up and there he was leaning on the railing looking down at me."

I tried to swallow the tightness in my throat.

"Did he . . . say anything?"

Harry shook his head slowly.

"He doesn't have to say anything," he said.

"Harry, you know that contract isn't . . ."

"Oh, why talk?" he said bitterly. "I signed and he wants payment."

For a long time I stood there without speaking. Then I put my hand on his shoulder.

"You want me to tell Harold to pitch somebody else today?" I asked him.

"No," he said, "I . . . I'm not going to let the team down again."

I patted his shoulder.

"All right, pop," I said.

The next hour was like the beginning of a nightmare when you're asleep, all the elements adding up until you suddenly realize you're getting the shakes. I could feel that while I was getting dressed. The chatter of the rest of the team sounded hollow and I kept looking over at Harry who still sat on the bench looking at his right arm, running his left hand over it again and again. I could feel it while we all moved through the tunnel to the dugout and the murmur of the people in the stands came down to us like far off sounds that frighten you even though you can't quite identify them. Then we came into the dugout and people started cheering.

I was putting on my equipment when I saw Harry standing by the stands talking to a man; a man in a summer suit with a woven hat that had a colored band. I felt my body go cold and I stood there fumbling with my shin guards, my eyes fastened on the face of the man Harry was talking to.

When Harry came back to the dugout his whole body shook. I went to him.

"What is it, what is it?" I whispered.

"I told you," he said in a terrified murmur. "He wants payment."

"Didn't you tell him about . . ."

He jerked his head with a nod. "I told him," he said. "He got mad. He said I was cheating him."

"And . . . ?"

His throat moved.

"That's all," he said.

"What?"

"He just . . . turned around and walked away," Harry said, his pupils pinpoints of jet.

"Then," I started, "then he's leaving you alone."

Harry didn't reply. He moved away and bent over the water cooler.

Ten minutes later we went out to warm him up. Everybody cheered and I saw Harry's body jolt at the sound. I glanced at the stands but I couldn't see the man, just a sea of red, happy faces.

Harry started throwing. I had trouble with my hands at first but then I saw that the ball was coming in good. Harry was fast and he had plenty of control. I started to relax. With every pitch that came in fast or curving or sinking and right in the strike zone the more excited I got. Until, finally, I jumped up and raced over to Harry. I clapped him on the back and I said, "You've licked him, pop!"

Minutes later. The captains went out, exchanged line-ups, the national anthem was sung and we were all in the field. Harry threw in some more warm-up pitches, the outfielders arranged themselves for the first batter. The umpire yelled *"Play Ball!"*

Johnny Morgan of the Yanks was first to bat. He got up to the plate and pumped a little. The umpire leaned over my shoulder. I gave Harry the signal. He shook it off. I chuckled and gave him the signal we'd worked out between us, the one that meant—*All right, play it any way you want, you bum.* And I grinned at him.

Harry went into his motion, pumped once, twice . . .

I was watching the ball so I didn't see. The first thing that got to me was Harry's scream ringing out over all the noise of the crowd. I jumped up with my heart jolting and the ball bounced off my chest guard. Women in the stands were screaming too. And, as I stood, I saw Harry paralyzed out there on the mound and staring at his arm.

It was lying on the ground. Still twitching.

Mirror, Mirror . . .

THIS IS ONE OF THOSE STORIES that begins as it ends. Except, of course, that identical words can mean two different things when their context alters. And the words are these:

She was one of those women who sit endlessly before mirrors and adore themselves. Let these silver backed glasses be considered the pool of Narcissus and you have pretty much the case of it. For should the truth out, these women who pose their hours away love nothing but themselves. Let there be husbands and homes and duties, yes—but let there be a wrinkle and the rest is forgotten in fretfulness and vain dismay. Give them largesse of affection, kindness, understanding, love—then give them praise about their looks and the subtler gifts will be ignored.

Such a woman then was Valerie Castle whose private sun rose and fell on matters facial. That she was married bore relation more to sustenance than to romance. She cared far more for tubes and jars of cosmetic application than for her husband John, a plain man inclined to bovine temper and unassailable adoration of his wife.

For she was a splendid figure of a woman and John counted himself joyously among those legions who serve as carpets for the beautiful. It is not that John Castle was stupid. His relative mark on finance belied this apparentness. He was merely indulgent to that point from which, once arrived at, no woman lets any man return.

Here then the elements: A husband puffing faithfully on the fire of his wife's vanity.

Here then the story.

One morning Valerie Castle awoke from fitful slumber,

trembling with the memory of a dream. The scene still clung with vivid fingers to her mind—Her, ugly with such ugliness as only women fearful of their beauty can imagine, forced to bear the cross of observation from a body of women through whose silent ranks she was compelled to walk—slowly.

She lay supine, the picture of beauty perturbed; aggravated to the very core by these nightly repetitions of a dream so unwholesome. It was most unfair, this rack of visions, this terrible release of fears from mental attic rooms. The unconscious mind, it was a beast to dally so with apprehensions.

Valerie Castle drew pretty fingers into pretty fists and sulked on mind's inhumanity to mind. Then her azure eyes grew full with fright. Was there significance to this—these similar dreams? Was she, perhaps unknowing it, looking at events to come?

A shudder ran down her milk white limbs. Nonsense, she abjured her scant used ration; it was only nerves sitting uneasy on a beleaguered throne of loveliness. Did not the concert pianist tremble for his hands, the artist for his eyes? Natural fear, no more. Should not beauty tremble lest, through horrible accident, she become the beast instead?

Of course; that was settled. Perhaps a few brief visits to an analyst to dismiss the tension and bring slumber once again. Something of that nature at any rate. She'd see, she'd see.

That annoyance taken in count, Valerie Castle rustled shimmering hair on pillow and eyed the clock.

Disturbed surprise lifted her well plucked eyebrows. Almost twelve already and not one iota of preparation yet for Mrs. Rigney's afternoon bridge and social tea. A sound of harried resolution sounded beneath Valerie's cold creamed neck. She simply *had* to retire earlier, that was all. Her lubricated lips grew firm. It was John with his exhausting, endlessly visiting business connections that made life so trying and adequate sleep so hard to acquire.

I knew a woman once, thought Valerie, who was the

beauty of her time; nationally noted, the enchantress of all men who had known her.

Well, that woman retained her stunning grace only so long as she slept twelve full hours a night in her own private bed. Once she had married and fallen heir to an hour consuming husband, her famous charm degraded markedly; she became that basest of the base—a sacrificing wife.

Well, by the heavens, nothing like that would ever happen to Valerie Castle! Let John but *breathe* the first syllable of a demand and he'd see sparks from her.

She nodded once in violent agreement with herself. Sound, completely sound. A woman should look after herself first; who else was there that cared? From genesis to exodus each woman stood upon a lonely battlefield, in combat for her rights. No kinsman succored, no liege raised arms in selfless aid and each apparent champion revealed himself a mercenary in the end.

Settled; done and done. Again the sky blue eyes of Valerie Castle moved, this time settling on the window of her world —a mirror; her personal hand mirror this. For moments she allowed her gaze to stir caressing on the convoluted tracery of silver which exacting craft had fashioned on its back. A stunning work of artisan detail, full worthy in its finished grace of all the beauty its other side reflected.

Fingers curled in satiny languor, Valerie Castle stretched an ivory arm. The canons of beauty demanded this ritual of critical regard promptly at the rising hour. No negligence was sanctioned, no laxity indulged. Loveliness must never be remiss is this, its primal duty. Devout, reverent, Valerie Castle obeyed the edicts of appearance.

Now the mirror passed in transit, now two perfect eyes beheld.

Now the cook, preparing breakfast biscuits, dropped a bowl of snow white batter on the floor, the maid gasped loudly and the right cheek of the butler twitched.

That suddenly had a scream of horror filled the house.

"I really thought my heart would stop it was so hideous," she said.

"You say it wasn't you in the mirror?"

The chapeaued trio sat apart in confidential huddle, their voices soft in stealthy conversation. Valerie Castle, firmly center staged, replied.

"It *wasn't* me," she said, "I don't know who it was. It was a *guignol* face, a *horrid* face, one of scarred distortion. The mouth curled up and down as though one side were smiling while the other frowned. A grisly patch of skin covered a third of one eye. The nose, in shape and hue, was very like a potato, newly dug. And the lips . . ."

Tea cups stood ignored, glacéd cakes neglected as the pair of women eyed a shuddering Valerie Castle.

"A frightening incident," said one.

"My sister once," the other said, "had a similar experience. She invariably saw reflected in all water the features of her Pekingese dog who had died quite horribly beneath the hooves of a runaway horse."

"What shall I do?" a distraught Valerie Castle asked. "It fills me with terror. I dare not look into another mirror lest I see that face again."

"You haven't looked into a mirror since you saw it?" asked one of the women.

"No," said Valerie Castle. "I fear to."

"But you say it did not last," the woman pointed out. "You say that following a moment's appearance, the face disintegrated as it were and there you saw your own again."

"Yes," said Valerie Castle, "that is true."

"Then it is nothing but an aberration," said the woman. "To be dealt with by a proper analyst."

Said the other woman, "Did the face resemble yours at all?"

"*Please,*" said Valerie Castle.

"I mean," the woman hastily amended, "as you might appear following terrible catastrophe."

Valerie leaned forward, beauty petrified.

"It is what I fear," she confessed in hollow voice. "What I cannot dismiss from mind."

"I do not believe in such nonsense," said the other woman. "Aberration of the psyche, no more. Work for an analyst, not a medium."

"I want to believe that," Valerie said. "I want desperately to believe that."

"I shall give you the name of my personal analyst," the woman declared. "I shall phone him this evening to let him know you are coming. But for now . . . your purse mirror."

"I dare not," murmured Valerie Castle, white gloved fingers trembling.

"You must," said the woman. "You know your face has not changed. To look is a requisite of cure. *Face the problem and the problem loses face.* It is a truism taught to me by Doctor Mott who is my analyst. Come, your mirror."

Slowly, shaking with premonitional chills, Valerie Castle opened up her purse and closed tense fingers on the mirror edge.

"Courage," said one woman.

"I could *never* look," said the other.

Valerie Castle did.

Although the maid might try as she proferred the cherry tarts, she could not half erase the look of most offensive curiosity from her face. As might be expected however, Valerie noted with disgust, John made not the slightest note of it. But then John was never of the sensitive variety. Bluntly unaware, that was his proper labeling.

Such waspish reflections stung at Valerie Castle's mind as she jabbed indifferent fork into her tart. I will not have the help surveying me with uncivil eyes, she thought, probing their scalpel glances in my back and whispering among themselves.

"This tart is admirable," said Mr. Castle.

Just because I screamed in my fright they eye me much as though my mind were visibly crumbling. I see no reason to abide the utter vulgarity of their inspection; I am not upon exhibit for their churlish eyes.

"This tart is admirable, my dear," said Mr. Castle.

The face I saw was nothing but a fleeting aberration, that is certain; a mental spot to be removed tomorrow morning by the analyst. The proof is clear: I saw no face except my own in the mirror from my purse. And, since that moment, I have looked in twenty different mirrors in this very house, seeing only what I always see, the pattern of my private features.

"My dear?"

For that single cry am I to be abused by loutish gapes? I find the situation more than . . .

"Dear?"

"What *is* it?" asked a petulant Valerie Castle.

"This tart is admirable. Did you think of it yourself?"

"Why do you ask me such a foolish question?" she replied. "You know I don't go near the kitchen."

"Oh. Well, I do . . . apologize . . . my dear. It is just that it is such an admirable tart."

If they continue staring as they do I shall be compelled to discharge them. There is no other way. I will tell John merely that I find them inefficient. There is no point in telling him of my experience, he lacks capacity to understand such things.

"What?" she said.

"Shall I ring for coffee?" he inquired.

"Really, do you have to *ask* me?" she replied in fine exasperation. "Ring for it if you wish."

With flickering smile John Castle rang and, in the kitchen,

the maid drew breath into her lungs and lifted up the heavy polished urn. She scrabbled backwards through the swinging door, then turned about and scuffed politely to the table end at which her mistress sat.

She lowered down the urn and moved away as Valerie grasped her cup and held it underneath the spigot. Then, as the coffee jetted black and steaming in the cup, Valerie's eyes moved up instinctively, as they invariably did when faced by any bright, reflecting surface.

Abruptly, nerveless fingers lost hold upon the handle and coffee torrented across the glossy oak to waterfall across the table edge. The spigot, still discharging, splashed smoky brew into the curving dish below it. John Castle started to his feet, eyes expansive with alarm.

Quickly Valerie Castle closed the spigot, quicker yet dropped damask napkin on the table and arose.

"Have you burned yourself, my love?" inquired a solicitously approaching Mr. Castle.

"It is nothing, nothing."

The footfalls of her tiny shoes moved rapidly beneath the alcove to the living room rug.

"My dear!" John Castle hurried in concerned pursuit.

"*Leave me alone!*" she cried, so that the servants heard again.

The clicking of her heels echoed sharply up the curving stair flight and did not cease until she sat in short-breathed silence in her room, hunched before the spacious mirror of her dressing table. Outside, in the hall, prowled a harried husband.

Was it just imagination aggravated by distortion in the urn reflection? Or had she truly seen that awful face again?

A fearful tightness held her ivory throat like strangling claws, her hands vibrated, helpless in her lap. Imagination or the truth?

She had to know.

"Valerie. *My dear.* Tell me what is wrong!"

Heart like pounding tympani in her breast, she raised her eyes and looked.

A moment later all there was within the mirror face was the converse picture of a woman's room. The woman herself lay senseless on the rug beneath debris of combs, brushes, tubes and jars. While talcum powder like a floury snow drifted silently across her outflung arm.

When she had finished her account, Doctor Mott had nodded purse lipped, hands still clasped upon his desk edge, portly thumbs still circling one another.

"So," he said, admiring her appearance.

"Miss Pettigrew has highly recommended you," said Valerie. "That is why I came."

Doctor Mott acknowledged this remark with rocking head nod.

"Just so," he said. Her clothes, he thought, they fit her flawlessly.

"You do not think it possible that . . ."

"That you really saw that face," he said, snapping back into his professional niche. "Why, yes of course. You saw it."

Valerie Castle shuddered, digging lacquered nails into her palms.

"Which is not at all to say the face was really there," completed Doctor Mott. "Discharge such possibility from your mind. The face exists but only in your id, you comprehend?"

"You mean it is not actual."

"Actual in your mind," said Doctor Mott, "seeded by obsession, nurtured by increasing phobia and ultimately harvested in this wracking vision. But please dismiss the thought that this sad episode has proved clairvoyance. No, not at all, my dear, it merely shows once more the torture chamber that we build within ourselves to grieve ourselves."

"You say obsession," Valerie replied. "Obsession over what?"

"Your looks, of course," said Doctor Mott. "To be precise, your fear of losing them."

"But *such* a face," said Valerie, "and in such terrible detail. How could my mind evolve a face so definite?"

"Who knows what care the machinations of the mind involve? Least of all myself for all my years of study. I know only this, the mind is diabolic in its sleight and dexterous invention. Believe me when I say that to create a face within a mirror is but child's play to a mind imbued."

"But how am I to cure it?" Valerie inquired. "Then, is it hopeless?"

"Not in the least," said beaming Doctor Mott. "Now to begin . . ."

The elevator slowly sank into its well, humming past the numbered floors. Valerie Castle stood within the falling cubicle, a smile compressed between her lips.

It was just as she had reasoned then, she thought, a fancy neurotic, a tendency disordered. Well, at least she'd had the wit to nip this cancerous malady in its bud. It would not be too long now. Doctor Mott's assurances had loosed the tension and a short prescribed assay into her subconscious would cure the rest.

She slid herself across the leather seat of her convertible, a smile of self possession asserted on her lips. How comforting it was to relegate the unknown to the known, to light a bulb of cognizance in the darkened room of rationless anxiety.

The situation was entirely explicable—should not beauty fear the blighting of its own perfection? A natural diffidence in any woman gifted with the dearest compliment of nature —a lovely visage.

Another smile of confidence as Valerie inserted shiny key

and twisted. The Cadillac motor coughed into euphonious combustion. The automatic gears revolved, the polished phaeton nudged away the curb and joined the shifting tapestry of traffic.

Now the mind of Valerie Castle turned to primal love.

Tomorrow night the banquet at the home of Mrs. Royal Arkwright. There was endless preparation to be made. The final fitting for her gown, the hours to be spent beneath the kneading fingers of the masseuse, the mudpack's ooze, the electric helmet of the hair machine, the file and orange stick of the manicurist. So much tiresome provision in exchange for blathering male dialogue and epicurean mélange. What merciless demands beauty really made upon its hapless possessor, came the not too irking rumination.

The traffic light now shifted orange caution to green allowance, the gears gnashed teeth, her Cadillac moved regally across the intersection, holding to the outer lane. Behind, a harried salesman sounded horn in his desire to pass.

A pity the entire morning had been wasted on analysis of mind, thought Valerie.

The salesman honked again, his ire in the ascendancy.

To recapitulate: At one, the fitting at Antoine's. At two ...

The horn, most urgent, tore her veil of meditation. Hardening eyes sought out the culprit in the rear view mirror. The mirror had been turned. It faced her.

"*No!*"

The cry that forced apart her shaking lips could not be heard in all the traffic noise. And no one saw her twist away in horror from the mirror nor witnessed how her hands ripped in mindless terror from the wheel.

What people saw was a rather nasty accident.

Light flickered in the blackness of the room as if the hidden operator had thrown his switch and started his projection. His lens was not in accurate adjustment though and fluttering arms and undulating faces were blurred to eye.

And yet, despite distortion, the scene was simple to identify. The paleness of the walls, the ashen costumes of the moving figures, the smell of calculated disinfection in the air. These things described precisely a hospital effect.

Ah, now the lens was slowly turned, the picture clarified. A smell? Great God, what picture had aroma, what film such three dimensional precision?

Her head jerked sideways on the pillow, eyes picking at the walls, the door, the windows, the somber faces of the nurse and interne. And, suddenly, the terror billowed; two pale hands moved searching to her face.

Which face was wrapped entire in bandaged strips.

"Oh, no." Her voice emerged a bubbling sibilance in the quiet room.

The intern and the nurse looked down into her stricken eyes which peered at them through loopholes in the gauze.

The intern held her wrist in pulsebeat estimation.

"So you are conscious now," he murmured.

"My face! Please tell me what has happened to my face!"

"You've been in quite an accident," the intern said, "the flying glass, you know."

"Oh, God, my face!"

The wares of half a florist's shop did not abate the twisting horror in her heart. Jewels, bon bons, gifts and loving husband smiles did not appease the ruthless tension of her nerves. Her only thought concerned that promised moment when the bandages would be undone, the mirror placed into her shaking hand. And every second passing, all the minutes ticking into hours only added to the trembling panic of suspense.

When she raised the mirror would she see—*that face?*

The day arrived. The surgical shears moved snipping through the bandage layers. Beside the bed stood waiting

Mr. Castle, smiling as he could, holding in his nervous hands the mirror for his wife. The doctor's face was grimly set. There was no sound within the room save that of scissors clicking razor jaws together.

And then the bandages were drawn away, Valerie Castle grabbed the mirror from her husband's hand and looked.

"Oh . . . *God*," she sobbed. "Thank God, thank God! I have not changed at all."

And then she looked up smiling to the face of Mr. Castle and saw the horror there.

She sits alone within her room, never stirring out, not in the street, not down the stairs, not even in the hall. A dozen separate surgeries have failed to repossess the beauty of her past. Her features only shift from one sad ugliness into the next.

And yet there is this other element.

For, in that moment when her bandages were taken off, she actually saw within the mirror the face she knew and so adored. And now, just every once so often, as she gazes in her mirror, her old face is reflected in all its perfect line and hue. Sometimes only for a second, other times for longer minutes; once it even lasted for an hour.

She never knows, you see, exactly when the shifting will occur, just when the mirror surface is to cloud, then show her long departed beauty once again. She dare not be away however lest she miss the moment. And so she has her meals placed on the table just outside her always bolted door. She eats and drinks and lives entirely in her room.

Which is, you see, the reason that I said this story ends as it begins except, of course, that similar words can mean two different things when context alters.

For Valerie Castle still remains one of those women who sit endlessly before their mirrors.

Well, perhaps it's not the same. If not, why, I apologize.

Then let me make amends by telling you about the ghost whose ectoplasm unexpectedly congealed thus rendering him a bowl of gelatine.

It seems that . . .

Two O'Clock Session

THE BREAKTHROUGH CAME AT TWO FORTY-ONE. Until that time, Maureen had done little more than repeat the bitter litany against her parents and brother.

"I have nothing to live for," she said then. "Absolutely nothing."

Dr. Volker didn't respond, but felt a tremor of excitement in himself. He'd been waiting for this.

He gazed at the young woman lying on his office couch. She was staring at the ceiling. What was she thinking? he wondered. He didn't dare to speak. He didn't want to break in on those thoughts, whatever they might be.

At last, Maureen spoke again. "I guess you didn't hear that," she said.

"I heard," Dr. Volker replied.

"No reaction then?" she asked, an edge of hostility in her voice. "No sage comment?"

"Like what?" he asked.

"Oh, God, don't start that again," she said. "Respond with an answer, not another goddamn question."

"I'm sorry," Dr. Volker said. "I didn't mean to make you angry."

"Well, it *did* make me angry! It made me—" Her voice broke off with a shuddering throat sound. "You don't care," she said then.

"Of course I care," he told her. "What have I ever done to make you think I don't care?"

"*I said I have nothing to live for.*" Maureen's tone was almost venomous now.

"And—?" he asked.

"What do you mean *and?*" she snapped.

"And what does that make you feel like?"

The young woman shifted restlessly on the couch, her face distorted by anger. "It makes me feel like *shit!*" she said. "Is that precise enough for you, God damn it! I feel like *shit!* I don't want to live!"

Closer, Volker thought. A shiver of elation laced across his back. He was glad the young woman was turned away from him. He didn't want her to know how he felt.

"And—?" he said again.

"Damn it to hell!" Maureen raged. "Is that all you can say?!"

"Did *you* hear what *you* said?" Volker asked as calmly as he could.

"About what? About having nothing to live for? About wanting to *die?*"

"You didn't use the word *die* before," he corrected.

"Oh, big deal!" she cried. "I apologize! I said I don't want to live! Anyone else would assume from that that I want to die! But not you!"

"Why do you want to die?" Volker winced a little. He shouldn't have said that.

Maureen's silence verified his reaction. It became so still in the office that he heard the sound of traffic passing on the boulevard. He cleared his throat hoping that he hadn't made a mistake and lost the moment.

He wanted to speak but knew that he had to wait. He stared at the young woman on the couch. Don't leave me now, he thought. Stay with it. *Please*. It's been such a long time.

The young woman sighed wearily and closed her eyes.

"Have you nothing more to say?" he asked.

Her eyes snapped open and she twisted around to glare at him. "If I said what I wanted to say, your hair would turn white," she said, almost snarling the words.

"Maureen," he said patiently.

"*What?*"

"My hair is already white."

Her laugh was a humorless bark of acknowledgment. "Yes, it is," she said. "You're old. And decrepit."

"And you're young?" he asked.

"Young and . . ." She hesitated. "Young and miserable. Young and lost. Young and empty. Young and cold, without hope. Oh, *God!*" she cried in pain. "I want to die! I want to die! I'm going to see to it!"

Dr. Volker swallowed dryly. "See to what?" he asked.

"God damn it, are you stupid or something?" she lashed out at him. "Don't you understand English?"

"Help me to understand," he said. His pulsebeat had quickened now. He was so close, so close.

Silence again. Oh, dear Lord, have I lost her again? he thought. How many sessions was it going to take?

He had to risk advancing. "See to what?" he asked.

The young woman stared at the ceiling.

"See to what, Maureen?" he asked.

"Leave me alone," she told him miserably. "You're no better than the rest of them. My father. My mother. My brother."

Oh, Christ! Volker clenched his teeth. Not the goddamn litany again!

"My father raped me, did you know that?" Maureen said. "Did I tell you that? Tell you that I was only seven when it happened? Tell you that my mother did nothing about it? That my brother laughed at me when I told him? Did I tell you that?"

Volker closed his eyes. Only about a thousand times, he thought.

He forced himself to open his eyes. "Maureen, you were on to something before," he risked.

"*What do you mean?*" she demanded.

Oh, no, he thought, chilled. But he couldn't stop now. "You said you wanted to die. You said—"

The young woman twitched violently on the couch, her head rolling to the right on the pillow, eyes closed.

"No!" Volker drove a fist down on the arm of his chair.

One more failure.

When the young woman sat up, he handed her a glass of water.

Jane Winslow drank it all in one, continuous swallow, then handed back the glass. "Anything?" she asked.

"Oh ..." He exhaled tiredly. "The usual. We're right on top of it, but she backs off. She just can't face it." He shook his head. "Poor Maureen. I'm afraid it's going to be a long, long time before she's free to move on." He sighed in frustration. "Are you ready for the next one?"

She nodded.

At three o'clock she lay back on the couch and drew in long, deep breaths. She trembled for a while then lay still.

"Arthur?" Dr. Volker said.

Jane Winslow opened her eyes.

"How are you today?"

"How *should* I be?" Arthur said bitterly.

Dr. Volker rubbed fingers over his eyes. Helping them was difficult. My God, how difficult. He had to keep trying though. He had no choice.

"So, how's life treating you, Arthur?" he asked.

And in Sorrow

W HITE IS COLD. Not just because it is the hard imper-
sonal glitter of winter. White is cold because it is
harsh and sterile. It stretches on endlessly, an impassive
blankness. White is cheerless; an antiseptic shade.

White was the color of the walls that day.

White in the laboratory where they had taken my life
force and isolated its parts.

White in the reception room with its furnishings of bright
tubular steel, polished and aloof; where I sat waiting for my
wife Patricia.

I tried to think of the money we were going to get; of all
our financial worries at last reduced to their proper pettiness. It was a good feeling in part.

Yet, exhausting those anxieties only left the rest larger.
In some ways it is almost a consolation to be absorbed in
money matters. It leaves no time for other concern.

And as I sat waiting, I thought of how it had begun; in our
apartment about one month before; May 10, 1975.

She stood facing the window. Angry words still hovered
above us. I stepped behind her, closed my fingers on her arms.

"Baby, let's not quarrel," I said.

She twisted a little in my hands.

"Oh, Davie," she said. "Why is it like this?"

No words could capture the reasons. I could only stroke
her arms and kiss her hair. She clasped her hands beneath
her chin and I watched the knuckles grow white.

"You'd think we were asking for the world or something,"
she said. "A little new furniture. A few new clothes . . ."

She sighed.

"And we want to have a baby," she said. "What do they call that; sterility of the budget?"

I had no answer. I felt ashamed to have promised once and not fulfilled.

"If I could sell an arm," I said seriously, "or a leg. Maybe my lab would like a . . ."

"Stop talking like that," she said peevishly, "that doesn't help."

I put my arms around her. She held on to my wrists tightly.

"You mustn't ever talk like that," she said quietly.

It was early evening. Up the block, the theatre marquee was flickering on into gaudy colors. In the street, boys were playing ball. Cars kept driving through center field and rolling over home plate.

"Honey," she asked, "can't we afford just one new living room chair? Just one?"

I exhaled a long loud breath.

"You know what we have in the bank as well as I do," I said. "We have to save something. We do want a baby some day don't we?"

"O-oh," she said, her voice rising in annoyance. "Why doesn't that fool lab pay you a decent salary?"

I took a deep breath and pulled my arms back. She turned quickly and pressed against me.

"I'm sorry," she said. "Davie, I'm sorry."

She kissed my cheek and we embraced.

"Money, money, money," she said. "Why is it so important? Why does it always spoil everything?"

"I don't know baby," I said. "I just don't know."

That was when I saw Ted's car turn into the block.

"Here comes our fair-haired scientist," I said.

"Where does he get off with a car like that?" she said.

★

Ted and I had both majored in the Biological Unit at Fort College. That was as far as the resemblance went. I was an assistant in a small medical lab in the city's downtown section. Ted had a high-paying position doing research in genetics at the DeMorgan Institute of Medical Research.

When he got out of the car, Pat turned to me.

"I look all right?" she asked.

"If you looked any better," I said, "I'd be afraid to let him in."

"Huh," she said and started away. I grabbed her wrist and pulled her back.

"Cut it out," she laughed. "I have to put lipstick on, not take it off."

"No," I said, kissing her neck. "No, I want you to look like the well-kissed wife when guests come calling."

We wrestled until the doorbell rang. Then she kissed me once and pulled away.

"You old rake," she said, going into the bedroom.

"That's me," I admitted.

I opened the door. Ted was a little taller than me. He had a young searching look, a head of blond hair cut to a springy fuzz and the build of a football star.

"Hello, Dave," he said, shaking my hand with his powerful grip.

"Enter," I said.

He came in and I waved him to a chair.

"Where's Patricia?" he asked.

"She'll be out in a second. What tears you away from the test tubes? Tired of bachelor meals?"

He shook his head with a smile.

"No," he said. "I'll tell you as soon as Patricia is here."

"All right."

I was making him a drink when Pat came in, her silky brunette hair combed and lips freshly painted with her delicate tint of lipstick.

"Don't get up Ted," she said. "What brings you here? Tired of bachelor meals?"

I grinned as I handed Ted his drink.

"You see what an original family we are," I said. He smiled thinly.

"I say something?" Pat said. "Make me one, Davie."

"Right away. That bachelor meals gag. I just pulled it before you came in."

"Well," she said. "That's what you get for making me take that fool course in Basic Telepathy at Fort."

"I knew you'd live to regret it. Here." I handed her the drink.

"Thank you."

I sat down in my chair and Pat rested on the arm.

"What's the deal, Ted?" I asked. I turned to Pat. "Our boy has something cooking," I told her.

"Oh?" she said. "What is it, Ted?"

"Well, uh," he said a little awkwardly, "I hope I put this just right. It's a little . . . uh . . ."

"Indecent?" I said.

His lips twitched into a nervous smile.

"Not at all," he said affirmatively, "not at all. It's just that . . . well, let me put it this way. How would you like to make five thousand dollars?"

"You put it the right way," I said.

"Five thousand?" Pat said incredulously. "Dollars?"

Ted laughed self-consciously.

"That's right," he said.

"Without murder?" she said.

"No, no," he said, perfectly serious in a second. "Strictly honest. I'm just a . . . well, you know. A little embarrassed to . . ."

He cleared his throat suddenly and sat up straight in the chair.

"We believe," he said, as though commencing a formal

lecture, "that we've succeeded in isolating the male gamete from the female."

"What!" I cried.

That was something we used to muse about at college, make vague conjectures over; strictly the stuff of dreams. I had always considered it beyond the practical means of science.

"My God," I said, stunned by it. "They've done it? That's incredible."

I leaned forward.

"How, Ted? How?"

"Well," he said, slowly and carefully, "it's really too complicated a procedure to explain. And, well, to be frank, I don't understand the whole thing myself. It's mainly due to a, uh, a centrifugal gimmick we worked out. But there are other factors; a complex mass of them."

"I'll bet," I said. "I'll just bet there are. My God would I . . ."

"Will you please let me in on this?" Pat said. "And kindly tell me where the five thousand dollars comes in."

"Baby," I said excitedly, "don't you see? If what Ted says is actually so, there'll be no more guesswork about sex in babies. If a couple wants a boy, they can have one. If they want a girl, they can have a girl."

"No kidding?" she said. "That's wonderful!"

"Well," Ted broke in hurriedly, "we . . . we aren't positive of course. We haven't tested it with human procreation. Naturally we can't be sure until we do. And . . ."

"You want us?" Pat asked. "Is that it?"

Ted hesitated a moment, then nodded slowly and uncertainly.

"Well," he said, "we, uh, we've been trying to locate a couple. We thought of advertising. Then . . . I mentioned you two. Well, uh . . ."

He shifted in the chair and ran a hand over his short-cropped hair.

"Since there's no danger involved to the best of my knowledge, why, uh, I thought it would give you a chance to, well, to have that baby you've spoken about so often and . . . well, make some money too, and . . ."

He grimaced.

"Look," he said, "I didn't mean to put it that way. It's just that . . ."

"Calm down Ted," Pat said. "You're not insulting us."

She turned and looked at me. I could see the excitement pouring over the edges. It was a rich uncle dying, a windfall, manna from heaven. I'm sure she didn't realize for a second how it would be to conceive her first child under such conditions.

I made Ted tell us more. Most of it Pat didn't understand. She fidgeted at my side and tried to be patient. But she couldn't hold her exuberance in. I knew she had already made up her mind.

When Ted had gone, she made me sit down again. She plopped on my lap and clasped her hands behind my neck, smiling happily.

"Oh, Davie," she said with a shiver of delight.

I smiled and kissed her flushed cheek.

"We'll do it, won't we?" she said. "Won't we, Davie?"

"Now listen to me, baby," I said.

I told her what it would be like; what she would have to go through; artificial insemination, months of being little better than a guinea pig, perhaps terrible shock to her mind and body.

It didn't impress her.

"Oh, but I can stand it," she kept insisting. "I can stand it once Davie. Just think of all we can do with five thousand dollars. And we'd be having our baby too. And not only that, we can even decide on whether it'll be a boy or a girl!"

In the end I convinced myself that the advantages far outweighed the loss of romance. As always, practicality made the big difference. We could pay our bills, refurnish the apartment, buy clothes, do any number of needed things. Moreover Ted had told us that the Institute would provide all necessary services up to and including the delivery period.

We sat in the living room that night without turning on the lights, her curled up into a warm bundle on my lap. We talked in happy whispers, while outside the flicker of the theatre marquee sprayed the building walls with blinking colors.

It was dark. She held on to me, her warm breath caressing my cheek.

"Davie," she murmured, "let's decide whether we should have a boy or a girl."

Then she suddenly hugged me and squealed in childlike abandon. "Isn't it wonderful," she said, "to decide for ourselves? Isn't it exciting?"

It seemed exciting.

Conception by remote control. Love from a test tube. When I think back on it I wonder how we could have allowed anything so passionless and ugly to enter our marriage.

I didn't have her in my arms. I wasn't caressing her or kissing her and, with my love, softening the bluntness into beauty. I was separated, sitting in a white-walled reception room, smoking nervously. And somewhere, far apart, my wife was conceiving our first child.

When she came out, she was pale, uneasy. Ted was at her side. I stood up and went to her.

She pressed her cheek against mine and I felt her fingers dig into my arm. She whispered:

"It was a little mathematical for a way to have a baby."

I tried to speak but I didn't know what to say. A dozen different endearments sprang into mind and jumbled together. I felt cold and strangely perturbed. I kissed her damp forehead and hugged her.

"Well, the worst is over," Ted said, with blatant cheerfulness. "Now you can pick up your check at the cashier's window."

"Fine," I said. "Fine."

But I didn't feel fine as we pushed through the swinging doors into the deathly quiet hall and started for the elevators. It all seemed fantastic and unreal.

Then I was holding the check in my hand and Pat was smiling at me like a frightened little girl. And the whole thing poured over me like lead and hardened into a brain-crushing shell.

It almost made my flesh crawl to fully realize that deep in my wife's body, cells were joining, mixing, forming the first amorphous pattern of our coming child. I almost felt outraged, betrayed, the butt of an unfaithful act.

Yet far worse than my own feeling I could sense the terror that gripped Pat. She was really so young, so unprepared. Normal conception would, in itself, have been enough of a shock for her. But *this* . . .

I wanted to have her alone, to hold her and soothe her and make up for the cruel way she'd had to receive her baby.

Down in the street I hailed a cab. After I gave the driver our address I put my arm around her. She fell against me, the breath catching in her throat. I felt her shudder and warm tears ran down my shirt front.

"Oh, Davie, Davie," she sobbed.

"Baby, don't," I begged.

She raised her face quickly and our mouths clung together in a desperate kiss. Then she rubbed her cheek over mine.

"Just this once," she murmured in a thin high-strung voice, "never again. I don't want to have any more babies that way. I want you there when it happens."

We held on to each other without a word.

After a while she calmed down. She sat up a little and took a compact out of her coat pocket; peered at her reflection quizzically.

"I'm going to be a mother," she said as if she couldn't believe it, "a mother."

She snapped the compact shut and looked straight ahead with eyes that glistened. I pulled her back. She pushed against me and slid her shaking hands under my jacket.

"Think of all we can do with that money," she said hastily. "It's all right just this once. It's not so bad now. It's . . ."

She shivered and pressed her face against my shoulder.

"It was so awful." I heard her muffled shaky voice.

I stroked her hair gently.

"Don't think about it baby," I said. "We'll both try to forget it."

"Yes," she said. "We'll think about new furniture and clothes and . . .

"Davie," she said.

"What is it, baby?"

She hesitated, fingering the lapel of my jacket with one hand. I heard her throat contracting.

"Nothing," she said.

"Tell me."

After a moment she said:

"Do you think we chose right?"

"We . . . decided on a boy didn't we?" I said.

"Yes, but . . . oh, I'm just silly," she said, throwing off the mood. "It's better to know right away. Now we don't have to worry about it all the time. Will it be a boy? Will it be a girl? We know."

The forced look of pleasure faded from her face. She willed it back. "Remember," she went on quickly as if afraid to let herself think, "remember how we used to laugh at my sister when they were having their babies? When they kept wondering whether they'd have a boy or a girl? Remember that?"

"I remember," I said.

She sighed. I don't think she meant to speak out loud. It seemed more a thought. She whispered:

"They had sort of fun though."

It was about a week later.

I woke up around four in the morning and saw that Pat wasn't lying beside me. I got up slowly and went in the living room. She was standing by the window looking up at the dimming circle of the moon.

"Oh," she said, with a start. "You frightened me."

"What's the matter," I asked. "Can't you sleep?"

She took hold of my hand and squeezed it.

"It's nothing; I'm all right."

"Come on. Tell me," I said, blinking my eyes to stay awake.

I sat down on my chair and pulled her down on my lap. She rested her head on my shoulder.

"Now," I said.

"I was thinking about little Igor," she said.

I chuckled sleepily.

"That's a fine name," I said. "Well, what about little Igor?"

She rubbed her hand over my chest.

"I was thinking we lost something."

"Lost? What?"

"Oh," she said, "There's something about ... about *not* knowing that's nice."

That woke me up a little. It was true. Uncertainty can be beautiful. It can be exciting. We had lost that.

"Are you sorry already?" I asked.

She lifted her head and kissed my cheek.

"No, no, darling," she said softly, "I'm not sorry. We always wanted a boy. I'd be silly to complain now just because there's no chance of me having a girl."

But there was something wistful in her voice as though she half hoped she might have a girl.

"I just hope they don't tell us more," she said.

"About what, baby?" I said, closing my eyes.

"I mean, I hope they don't tell us any more about Igor. I don't want to know. I think it would be awful to know."

I tightened my arms around her and rested my head against hers.

"Don't worry baby," I said yawning. "All we know is that it'll be a boy. There's still plenty of mystery left."

She sighed and tugged me.

"Sure there is," she said. "Plenty of it."

Then she got up and tugged me to my feet.

"Come on, sleepyhead," she whispered.

It was after a month that Ted came.

It was colder and he had a briefcase with him. Otherwise, it seemed as though his last visit were being repeated. I made him a drink. Pat came out of the bedroom, hair combed, lips repainted. She sat on the arm of my chair.

"Hello Ted," she said.

"Hello," he said. "I . . . I see you've redone the apartment."

"Do you like it?" she said. "Little Igor paid for it."

"Who? Oh, are you going to name . . ."

"How do you like that?" Pat went on. "Most parents have to wait for twenty years before their kids start to pay off. Ours isn't even born yet and already he's redecorated the apartment."

Her lips were pressed together into a tight humorless smile. I squeezed her arm as Ted glanced at me, lost for something appropriate to say.

"I was only kidding," Pat said.

"Oh," said Ted. "I . . . I . . ."

"What's the briefcase for?" she asked.

Ted cleared his throat as he unzipped the top jerkily.

"Well," he said, "I think I have something here you'll find . . . well, interesting."

While he was bent over the case I turned Pat toward me and looked into her eyes. Her face was a mask of calm. She smiled at me quickly and, bending over suddenly, she kissed me on the cheek. Her fingers tightened on my shoulder.

Ted was waiting patiently when she finally straightened up.

"'Scuse it," Pat said.

A half smile flickered over his lips.

"Say," he said, "I hope those tests we're giving you don't, well, disturb you."

Pat hesitated. Then she said:

"Oh, they're grand."

Ted didn't get the sarcasm. He was satisfied.

"They try to be tactful," he said. "You know."

"I know."

She pointed quickly to the sheaf of papers on his lap.

"What are those?" she asked.

She'd only spoken to me once about the examinations and tests. But I knew she hated them.

Ted grinned.

"Want me to tell you about your baby?" he asked, almost shyly.

Pat's empty smile was gone. She pressed her hands together.

"Our baby?" she said.

"Yes," he said. "We have almost all the facts now, excluding environmental contingencies, of course."

"What are you saying?" she asked.

She turned to me.

"I don't understand," she said in a sharp disturbed voice.

"What do you mean, Ted?" I asked, afraid of his answer. "Are you telling us you know more than just the sex of our baby?"

"Why, of course," he said as if astounded at our lack of comprehension. "Why, we know almost everything about him."

"Oh, my God," I heard Pat say under her breath. Ted was looking at me. He didn't hear her.

"This is big," he said. "Darn big. The embryonic period hardly completed and yet already we have lists and lists of figures on the baby."

I glanced hurriedly at Pat. She might have been hypnotized. She was gazing at Ted without blinking, her lips slightly parted, her hands clasped and motionless in her lap.

I started to speak but Ted had already picked up a sheet.

"Of course it's to be a boy," he said with crushing finality. "You already know that yourself."

"Of course," Pat said. "That's just child's play."

She shuddered but Ted still didn't notice. He kept looking at his papers. I tightened my arm around her. I could almost feel the revulsion sweeping over her. We had made a mistake. We knew it with terrible clarity. There was no need to speak of it. Words couldn't have made the feeling any clearer or stronger. The horror of foreknowledge is beyond expression.

"Well, I won't go into all the details," Ted started talking again. "You wouldn't be interested in a good deal of it. Probably most of it would bore you."

Certainly! The thought cried out in my head. It's only our baby. That's a very boring subject.

"Probable weights by week during pregnancy, figures on general-specific, anterior-posterior, central-peripheral sequences, development of muscle, tissue, so on, so on."

He went on telling us about things we wouldn't be interested in; the way our child's body was forming itself, expanding, developing, the unfelt heartbeats already throbbing energy through its living structure. He rattled off figures in a bored voice.

Pat slid nervous hands over her forearms. I felt a dryness in my throat. I wanted to stop him, to scream: You idiot! Do you realize what you're doing? Do you know you're talking about our child? Do you know that you're dissecting him right before our eyes?

Ted glanced over another sheet.

"Oh," he said lightly. "This should interest you."

He nodded to himself.

"The boy," he said, "will have blue eyes and be blond like his father."

"Blue?" Pat said weakly. "Blue eyes?"

"Mmm-hmm. He'll weigh approximately seven and a quarter pounds at birth; barring environmental contingencies, of course. At your present rate of bodily development. If you . . ."

"That's enough!" I said.

His mouth remained open. A look of mystification crossed his smooth young features.

"What?" he said vaguely.

"Excuse me," Pat said. She got up and hurried from the room. The bedroom door shut noisily behind her.

Ted sat there holding his papers.

"What's wrong?" he asked.

I got up.

"Ted, will you go, please. I'm not throwing you out so don't get offended. But Pat is upset."

"Well . . ."

He slid the papers painstakingly into his briefcase until I could have hurled him through the window. He looked hurt. He'd been hoping for a great reaction to his list of figures. You could see that in his face. He hadn't expected this.

At the door he turned.

"Look," he said, pointing to the case, "this wasn't what upset her was it?"

"It's all right," I said, opening the door.

I ushered him out.

"I thought you'd be anxious to learn all about the baby," he said. "I thought . . ."

"Don't worry about it," I said hurriedly.

He went out, his face a picture of confused disappointment.

"Well," he said as I closed the door behind him. I heard his slow hesitant steps in the hallway.

I went to the bedroom quickly, my mind filled with sudden resentment at the plight she was in. I thought that there was a mystery to birth that we had lost; a wonderful and enchanting mystery. I was thinking that to solve it is to destroy it.

She was by the window. When I stepped behind her and put my arms on her shoulders I heard her talking to herself. She was staring at the light Sunday afternoon sky.

"Blue," she was whispering. "They're going to be blue."

Five months.

One cloudy evening I came home from work and found that Pat wasn't in the living room where she usually was reading. She wasn't in the kitchen either.

She was sitting in the bedroom, slumped down on the bed looking at the floor. She wore a loose housecoat over her widening body.

She looked up as I came in, her face stark with a helpless despair.

"Baby, what's the matter?" I asked.

"Don't call me baby," she said quietly, without rancor. "I'm not a baby anymore."

I sat down by her side and put my arm around her. As I kissed her cheek, I noticed a large envelope on the floor. I bent over and picked it up.

"DeMorgan Institute of Medical Research," it read in the upper left hand corner.

I pulled out the smooth square of paper inside. It was a color drawing of a little boy about four years old.

He had blue eyes and blond hair.

I felt my scalp tighten, my fingers twitched.

"No," I said.

"That's *him*," she said in a flat tone that droned from her throat. "That's what he'll look like when he's four. He's not even born yet but that's what he'll look like when he's four."

She shivered with nervous breath.

"Barring environmental contingencies of course," she said slowly and cruelly.

"What's the matter with them!" I said angrily. "I told them we didn't want any more predictions! I told Ted a hundred times. What's the matter with him?"

"They probably thought we'd enjoy seeing what our little boy will look like when he's four," she said.

I put down the picture and slid my arm around her.

"Take it easy," I said.

"I've been thinking about it all day," she said. "I've been here thinking about it. Why didn't they send us a picture of what he'll look like when he's forty? Then we wouldn't have to bother looking at him at all. We could just leave him in a corner and forget about him."

"Baby," I said. "It's all a guess, just a prediction. They can't possibly know exactly what he'll look like and how he'll think and what his reaction will be to everything. There's no way they can know. Don't you see that?"

"They know," she said. "They know everything."

"They don't," I argued. "They can't foresee accidents, they can't . . ."

I stopped short, my heart jolting. She had gasped. She was staring at me with wide eyes. Her coldness had gone, the shell had cracked.

"I didn't mean that," I said. But she didn't listen.

"What if he dies?" she said in a low terrified voice. "What if he dies when he's born!"

"He won't!"

She snatched up the picture and looked at it in a fascination of horror.

"Then this will be the picture of a ghost," she said. "A ghost of a little boy who never even lived."

She turned it over suddenly and closed her eyes.

"He's a ghost already," she said.

"Stop it," I told her.

She ran shaking hands over her stomach and the portrait fluttered to the floor.

"What does he think of it?" she murmured. "He doesn't like it either. He must hate everybody; telling him when to be born and how much to weigh and what color eyes to have and how smart to be. Telling him what he can learn and what he can't learn and how strong he'll be and how weak he'll be. He must hate us. He must . . ."

Suddenly her body jerked convulsively and she sat up straight, her mouth molded into a dark square of fright.

"He's kicking me!" she cried. "He's mad at me. He hates me! Davie!"

She threw herself against me and clung to me.

"He's kicking me," she sobbed. "Tell him to stop kicking me. Oh, please. Please, it hurts so. Stop! Make him stop kicking me!"

Words jumbled and failed in my throat. I ran my hands over her hair, tried to hold her so tightly that she couldn't tremble. I watched the hot tears running over her cheeks.

And while I held her, I happened to look down at the portrait. My son gazed up at me. A quiet bemused smile lifted the ends of his delicate mouth. He seemed to be listening to the raindrops which were beginning to spatter against the window panes.

Seven months. She never went out. She sat by the window and watched the cars pass, watched the bundled up children play in the cold street. She pressed her forehead against the window sometimes until the freezing glass numbed her flesh. Then she would lean back and rub her forehead slowly with a still quiet face.

One night I came home from work and she didn't greet me. And just the lack of that small act of turning around to say hello suddenly pointed up how terribly she had changed. I saw how sudden, how frightening the loss of youth can be.

I stood by the door and, in the wall mirror, I looked at her face. It was blank and lost. Her unkempt brown hair straggled over her shoulders. She sat limply and motionless, staring out at the evening sky.

I put my hands on her shoulders and bent over to kiss her.

"Darling," I said.

She didn't answer. I sat on the chair arm and put my arm around her. I didn't know what to talk about. Only the baby was important now. Everything else faded away into obscurity.

And yet I couldn't speak of the child. For I almost dreaded him. He seemed like some terrible stranger who had forced his life from Pat and myself, who had torn his body from hers and would soon reveal himself, alien and cruel.

"What did you do today?" I asked.

She didn't say anything.

"How did . . ." I said.

"Our scientist was here today," she interrupted listlessly.

My muscles tightened in fury.

"I told him to leave you alone!"

"They paid us money," she said without feeling. "We haven't any choice."

"He doesn't have to come and torture you. That isn't part of the experiment."

"They paid us money," she said. "We have no rights. We sold our lives to them."

I kept waiting for her voice to rise, to sink, to tremble, to do anything but remain on that dull monotonous level. Her terrible dispassion was frightening.

"Baby . . ."

But I couldn't call her that now. Not just because she told me not to. Somehow it didn't fit any more.

"Darling," I said. "It's only about two months now and then . . ."

"The birth labor will commence at 7:15 p.m. on the day of March 28, 1976."

She said it as though she were reading a time table.

"Pat."

"The rhythmic contractions will continue intermittently for five hours and seventeen minutes," she went on, her voice spilling out like the mechanical croak of a robot.

"Stop torturing yourself."

"At precisely 32 minutes after midnight on March 29, 1976, the child's head will . . ."

"Pat, stop it!"

"The child's head will . . ."

I grabbed her arm and squeezed it. She stopped. She twisted her head around and dug her nails into her palms.

"Excluding environmental contingencies, of course," she sobbed bitterly.

Then, abruptly, she drove a fist down on her right leg.

"I'm a factory," she cried. "They tell me what to make and I make it. I might as well be making an adding machine in my stomach!"

She tried to stand up, but she was off balance, she was too heavy. She fell back in the chair and began to cry.

It was like that all the time. She held it in, grew increasingly bitter. Then she broke down. And when that was over she was angry and reproachful again until the next breakdown. Day after day, week on week, beginning so far back I had forgotten the day.

I held her against me, her body wracked by helpless sobbing. Every time she cried it was less and less human, less controlled. It was no longer the delicate weeping of the girl I had married. It was the shattered outcry of a person denuded of all hope. It was broken and defeated, the last heartbroken revolt in darkness.

And every time she wept I told myself that it was the last time; dreading that I was right; that after that time she would no longer be able to cry. That she would lose her capacity for sorrow and become a cold unexpressive machine. Or worse.

The eighth month.

To herself, to the walls, to the universe, thin-lipped and sullen.

"Why can't it be a girl? What can't it . . ."

She couldn't remain still for a moment. I never knew what she did in the daytime. But in the evening and night she would pace the floor heavily, stand by the window a minute or so, shifting her awkward weight from one foot to the other, her hands clenching and unclenching at her sides.

Then she'd walk slowly and ponderously into the kitchen. I'd hear her running the water in the darkness, talking to herself. I couldn't make out the words. But they were always the same.

"Why can't it be a girl?"

I'd get up to speak, to try and comfort her. But she'd brush past me and go into the bedroom. I'd find her looking at the portrait. One day she had sketched in long hair with vengeful pencil strokes. I never tried to erase it.

She'd drop the picture on the floor and go back in the living room. Once more she'd stare out through the window, her shoulders twitching at the slightest noise, her fingers opening and closing together in monotonous rhythm.

She never wanted to go out. She didn't want to play cards or read or even talk to me. She hardly ever answered me. She was almost mute except for her one phrase.

If I woke up late at night I would hear the rustle of the blankets as she slowly rubbed her stomach. And if I turned on the bedside lamp I would see her staring at the ceiling with wide-open eyes, her lips forming the soundless phrase again and again.

"Why can't it be a girl?"

I tried to soothe, to calm, to make her speak. But she was always impassive now. It grew worse by the day. She wouldn't sob or cry anymore. It was all bound up inside of her. And though her eyes glistened, no tears would ever fall.

It was the ninth month.

I hurried up the steps anxiously the evening of March 25, 1976. In four days the child would be born.

I unlocked the door and stepped into our apartment.

I stood in the vestibule, dumbfounded.

The living room was brightly lit. In the center of the rug, the folding table was set gaily with a snowy cloth and napkins. In the glow of two red candles, dishes, glasses and silverware sparkled.

Pat was standing by the table. She looked up as I came in. Her hair was combed out, her makeup put on with meticulous care. She wore a light clean housedress around her swollen form.

"Hello, darling," she said lightly. She came over to me with quick waddling steps and kissed my cheek.

"I'm so glad you came early," she said. "The roast is just right now. You sit down and it'll be ready in a jiffy."

I watched her bustle into the kitchen. I put down my paper and hat in the vestibule and went in the bathroom to wash up. I felt my heart beating rapidly. My hands shook as I rubbed soap on them.

I sat down at the table, afraid to speak. I didn't know why she was so happy and I was afraid I'd say something to shatter the whole moment for her.

She set down a dripping brown roast on the table.

"There!" she said triumphantly. "Isn't that pretty?"

I nodded weakly.

"Yes," I muttered. "It's beautiful."

A silly laugh bubbled up in her throat as she sat down. She insisted on carving. I watched her and felt a shiver run through my body. I suddenly looked into her eyes. She glanced up at me and I lowered my gaze quickly and drank some water. I choked on it. She giggled. I put my hands on my lap to keep her from seeing how they shook.

She filled my plate, chattering on about what she'd done all day, asking me what I'd done at the lab, not waiting for me to answer. I ate in silence as she talked and talked. She never mentioned the baby once. My muscles felt like taut wires.

Then she suddenly paused. It was so silent that I looked up at her.

She was smiling like a little girl withholding some magnificent surprise.

"Guess what?" she blurted out, dropping her fork on her plate.

"What?"

"I'm going to have a girl!"

I gaped at her without comprehension.

"You're going to have a . . ."

"A girl!" she cried with a toss of her head.

I felt something well up inside of me. A rush of incomparable joy filled my mind.

They were wrong!

"You mean they haven't given you a boy?" I babbled anxiously. "You mean they made a mistake. They . . ."

"Yes!" she laughed. "Isn't that wonderful?"

I felt as though I would scream with happiness. I grabbed her hand and kissed it. I looked at her flushed happy face.

"When did this happen?" I asked quickly. "Did Ted tell you? When did they find out?"

"Oh," she said, "they don't know yet."

I felt as if I'd been kicked violently in the stomach.

All the excited warmth drained out of me. A shudder ran down through my body.

"They don't . . ."

"Darling," she said, a hysterical ring rising in her voice, "they don't have to tell me. After all who's having this baby, them or me? Who'd know better than me? I know I'm going to have a girl."

I felt numb. Every sight was gone but that of her unnaturally bright face, every sound disappeared but that of her voice bubbling on and on without pause.

"And she's not having blue eyes either. She's going to have brown eyes. I don't like blue eyes. You don't care for blue eyes that much, do you honey? I don't. And no blond hair either. Never mind blond hair anyway. What's the difference as long as she has hair."

She laughed loudly in that forced excited way.

"Darling," she said, taking my hand in her shaking fingers. "Darling, you don't mind if it isn't a boy do you? It can't be that important to you, can it? You don't mind if it's a girl do you, darling? Do you?"

Her eyes were glittering now.

I closed my hand over hers and tried to keep myself together.

"I don't mind," I said hoarsely.

"Oh, you're so sweet," she cried happily. "And she'll be beautiful. Really she will darling. You'll see. She'll have long brown hair and she'll be beautiful. You'll like that, won't you? Won't you, darling? Call me baby. Call me that."

"Yes . . . baby," I whispered.

She smiled tenderly.

"I know how you feel," she said. "I felt the same way when I knew it wasn't going to be a boy."

She looked at my plate.

"Oh, eat your dinner, honey," she said. "Oh, wait till you see what I made for dessert. Will you be surprised. Go ahead darling. Eat."

I ate. The food stuck in my throat. It felt like lead in my stomach. My hands shook. I could hardly hold the knife and fork. I felt tears running down my cheeks. I watched her eat, tried to smile back when she looked up, her eyes bright and wild, her hands trembling with excitement.

I kept hearing words in my mind, words that I had long forgotten. Over and over they repeated themselves.

"And in sorrow thou shalt bring forth children.

"And in sorrow . . ."

The Prisoner

WHEN HE WOKE UP HE WAS LYING ON HIS RIGHT SIDE. He felt a prickly wool blanket against his cheek. He saw a steel wall in front of his eyes.

He listened. Dead silence. His ears strained for a sound. There was nothing.

He became frightened. Lines sprang into his forehead.

He pushed up on one elbow and looked over his shoulder. The skin grew taut and pale on his lean face. He twisted around and dropped his legs heavily over the side of the bunk.

There was a stool with a tray on it; a tray of half-eaten food. He saw untouched roast chicken, fork scrapes in a mound of cold mashed potatoes, biscuit scraps in a puddle of greasy butter, an empty cup. The smell of cold food filled his nostrils.

His head snapped around. He gaped at the barred window, at the thick-barred door. He made frightened noises in his throat.

His shoes scraped on the hard floor. He was up, staggering. He fell against the wall and grabbed at the window bars above him. He couldn't see out of the window.

His body shook as he stumbled back and slid the tray of food onto the bunk. He dragged the stool to the wall. He clambered up on it awkwardly.

He looked out.

Grey skies, walls, barred windows, lumpy black spotlights, a courtyard far below. Drizzle hung like a shifting veil in the air.

His tongue moved. His eyes were round with shock.

"Uh?" he muttered thinly.

He slipped off the edge of the stool as it toppled over. His right knee crashed against the floor, his cheek scraped against the cold metal wall. He cried out in fear and pain.

He struggled up and fell against the bunk. He heard footsteps. He heard someone shout.

"Shut up!"

A fat man came up to the door. He was wearing a blue uniform. He had an angry look on his face. He looked through the bars at the prisoner.

"What's the matter with *you?*" he snarled.

The prisoner stared back. His mouth fell open. Saliva ran across his chin and dripped onto the floor.

"Well, well, well," said the man, with an ugly smile. "So it got to you at last, haah?"

He threw back his thick head and laughed. He laughed at the prisoner.

"Hey, Mac," he called. "Come 'ere. This you gotta see."

More footsteps. The prisoner pushed up. He ran to the door.

"What am I doing here?" he asked. "Why am I here?"

The man laughed louder.

"Ha!" he cried. "Boy, did you crack."

"Shut up, will ya?" growled a voice down the corridor.

"Knock it off!" the guard yelled back.

Mac came up to the cell. He was an older man with greying hair. He looked in curiously. He saw the white-faced prisoner clutching the bars and staring out. He saw how white the prisoner's knuckles were.

"What is it?" he asked.

"Big boy has cracked," said Charlie. "Big boy has cracked wide open."

"What are you talking about?" asked the prisoner, his eyes flitting from one guard's face to the other. "Where am I? For God's sake, where am I?"

Charlie roared with laughter. Mac didn't laugh. He looked closely at the prisoner. His eyes narrowed.

"You know where you are, son," he said quietly. "Stop laughing, Charlie."

Charlie sputtered down.

"Man I can't help it. This bastard was so sure he wouldn't crack. Not *me* boy," he mimicked, "I'll sit in that goddamn chair with a smile on my face."

The prisoner's greyish lips parted.

"What?" he muttered. "What did you say?"

Charlie turned away. He stretched and grimaced, pushed a hand into his paunch.

"Woke me up," he said.

"What chair?" cried the prisoner. "What are you talking about?"

Charlie's stomach shook with laughter again.

"Oh, Christ, this is rich," he chuckled. "Richer than a Christmas cake."

Mac went up to the bars. He looked into the prisoner's face. He said, "Don't try to fool us, John Riley."

"Fool you?"

The prisoner's voice was incredulous. "What are you talking about? My name isn't John Riley."

The two men looked at each other. They heard Charlie plodding down the corridor talking to himself in amusement.

Mac turned aside.

"No," said the prisoner. "Don't go away."

Mac turned back.

"What are you trying to pull?" he asked. "You don't think you'll fool us, do you?"

The prisoner stared.

"Will you tell me where I am?" he asked. "For God's sake, tell me."

"You know where you are."

"I tell you . . ."

"Cut it, Riley!" commanded Mac. "You're wasting your time."

"I'm not Riley!" cried the prisoner. "For God's sake, I'm not Riley. My name is Phillip Johnson."

Mac shook his head slowly.

"And you was going to be so brave," he said.

The prisoner choked up. He looked as though he had a hundred things to say and they were all jumbled together in his throat.

"You want to see the priest again?" asked Mac.

"Again?" asked the prisoner.

Mac stepped closer and looked into the cell.

"Are you sick?" he asked.

The prisoner didn't answer. Mac looked at the tray.

"You didn't eat the food we brought," he said. "You asked for it and we went to all that trouble and you didn't eat it. Why not?"

The prisoner looked at the tray, at Mac, then at the tray again. A sob broke in his chest.

"What am I doing here?" he begged. "I'm not a criminal, I'm . . ."

"Shut up for chrissake!" roared another prisoner.

"All right, all right, pipe down," Mac called down the corridor.

"Whassa matter?" someone sneered. "Did big boy wet his pants?"

Laughter. The prisoner looked at Mac.

"Look, will you listen?" he said, the words trembling in his throat.

Mac looked at him and shook his head slowly.

"Never figured on this did you, Riley?" he said.

"I'm not Riley!" cried the man. "My name is Johnson."

He pressed against the door, painful eagerness on his features. He licked his dry lips.

"Listen," he said. "I'm a scientist."

Mac smiled bitterly and shook his head again.

"Can't take it like a man, can you?" he said. "You're like all the rest for all your braggin' and struttin'."

The prisoner looked helpless.

"Listen," he muttered hoarsely.

"You listen to *me*," said Mac. "You have two hours, Riley."

"I told you I'm not . . ."

"Cut it! You have two hours. See if you can be a man in those two hours instead of a whining dog."

The prisoner's face was blank.

"You want to see the priest again?" Mac asked.

"No, I . . ." started the prisoner. He stopped. His throat tightened.

"Yes," he said. "I want to see the priest. Call him, will you?"

Mac nodded.

"I'll call him," he said. "In the meantime, keep your mouth shut."

The prisoner turned and shuffled back to the bunk. He sank down on it and stared at the floor.

Mac looked at him for a moment and then started down the hall.

"Whassa matter?" called one of the prisoners mockingly. "Did big boy wet his pants?"

The other prisoners laughed. Their laughter broke in waves over the slumped prisoner.

He got up and started to pace. He looked at the sky through the window. He stepped up to the cell door and looked up and down the hall.

Suddenly he smiled nervously.

"All right," he called out. "All right. It's very funny. I appreciate it. Now let me out of this rat trap."

Someone groaned. "Shut up, Riley!" someone else yelled.

His brow contracted.

"A joke's a joke," he said loudly. "But now I have to . . ."

He stopped, hearing fast footsteps on the corridor floor. Charlie's ungainly body hurried up and stopped before the cell.

"Are you gonna shut up?" he threatened, his pudgy lips outthrust. "Or do we give you a shot?"

The prisoner tried to smile.

"All right," he said. "All right, I'm properly subdued. Now come on." His voice rose, "Let me out."

"Any more crap outta you and it's the hypo," Charlie warned. He turned away.

"Always knew you was yellow," he said.

"*Listen* to me, will you?" said the prisoner. "I'm Phillip Johnson. I'm a nuclear physicist."

Charlie's head snapped back and a wild laugh tore through his thick lips. His body shook.

"A nu-nucleeeee . . ." His voice died away in wheezing laughter.

"I tell you it's true," the prisoner shouted after him.

A mock groan rumbled in Charlie's throat. He hit himself on the forehead with his fleshy palm.

"What won't they think of next?" he said. His voice rang out down the corridor.

"You shut up too!" yelled another prisoner.

"Knock it off!" ordered Charlie, the smile gone, his face a chubby mask of belligerence.

"Is the priest coming?" he heard the prisoner call.

"Is the priest coming? Is the priest coming?" he mimicked. He pounded on his desk elatedly. He sank back in the revolving chair. It squeaked loudly as he leaned back. He groaned.

"Wake me up once more and you'll get the hypo!" he yelled down the corridor.

"Shut up!" yelled one of the other prisoners.

"Knock it off!" retorted Charlie.

The prisoner stood on the stool. He was looking out through the window. He watched the rain falling.

"Where am I?" he said.

Mac and the priest stopped in front of the cell. Mac motioned to Charlie and Charlie pushed a button on the control board. The door slid open.

"Okay, Father," said Mac.

The priest went into the cell. He was short and stout. His face was red. It had a kind smile on it.

"Say, wanna hand me that tray, Father?" Mac asked.

The priest nodded silently. He picked up the tray and handed it to Mac.

"Thank you kindly, Father."

"Certainly."

The door shut behind the guard. He paused.

"Call out if he gets tough," he said.

"I'm sure he won't," said Father Shane, smiling at the prisoner who was standing by the wall, waiting for Mac to go.

Mac stood there a moment.

"Watch your step, Riley," he warned.

He moved out of sight. His footsteps echoed down the corridor.

Father Shane flinched as the prisoner hurried to his side.

"Now, my son . . ." he started.

"I'm not going to hit you, for God's sake," the prisoner said. "Listen to me, Father . . ."

"Suppose we sit down and relax," said the priest.

"What? Oh, all right. All right."

The prisoner sat down on the bunk. The priest went over and picked up the stool. Slowly he carried it to the side of the bunk. He placed it down softly in front of the prisoner.

"Listen to me," started the prisoner.

Father Shane lifted a restraining finger. He took out his

broad white handkerchief and studiously polished the stool surface. The prisoner's hands twitched impatiently.

"For God's sake," he entreated.

"Yes," smiled the priest, "for His sake."

He settled his portly form on the stool. The periphery of his frame ran over the edges.

"Now," he said comfortingly.

The prisoner bit his lower lip.

"Listen to me," he said.

"Yes, John."

"My name isn't John," snapped the prisoner.

The priest looked confused.

"Not . . ." he started.

"My name is Phillip Johnson."

The priest looked blank a moment. Then he smiled sadly. "Why do you struggle, my son? Why can't you . . ."

"I tell you my name is Phillip Johnson. Will you listen?"

"But my son—"

"Will you?"

Father Shane drew back in alarm.

"Will you shut that bastard up!" a voice said slowly and loudly in another cell.

Footsteps.

"Please don't go," begged the prisoner. "Please stay."

"If you promise to speak quietly and not disturb these other poor souls."

Mac appeared at the door.

"I promise, I promise," whispered the prisoner.

"What's the matter now?" Mac asked. He looked inquisitively at the priest.

"You wanna leave, Father?" he asked.

"No, no," said Father Shane. "We'll be all right. Riley has promised to . . ."

"I told you I'm not . . ."

The prisoner's voice broke off.

"What's that?" asked the priest.

"Nothing, nothing," muttered the prisoner. "Will you ask the guard to go away?"

The priest looked toward Mac. He nodded once, a smile shooting dimples into his red cheeks.

Mac left. The prisoner raised his head.

"Now, my son," said Father Shane. "Why is your soul troubled? Is it penitence you seek?"

The prisoner twisted his shoulders impatiently.

"Listen," he said. "Will you listen to me. Without speaking? Just listen and don't say anything."

"Of course, my son," the priest said. "That's why I'm here. However..."

"All right," said the prisoner. He shifted on the bunk. He leaned forward, his face drawn tight.

"Listen to me," he said. "My name isn't John Riley. My name is Phillip Johnson."

The priest looked pained.

"My son," he started.

"You said you'd listen," said the prisoner.

The priest lowered his eyelids. A martyred print stamped itself on his face.

"Speak then," he said.

"I'm a nuclear physicist. I..."

He stopped.

"What year is this?" he asked suddenly.

The priest looked at him. He smiled thinly.

"But surely you..."

"Please. *Please*. Tell me."

The priest looked mildly upset. He shrugged his sloping shoulders.

"1954," he said.

"What?" asked the prisoner. "Are you sure?" He stared at the priest. "Are you sure?" he repeated.

"My son, this is of no purpose."

"1954?"

The priest held back his irritation. He nodded.

"Yes, my son," he said.

"Then it's true," said the man.

"What, my son."

"Listen," said the prisoner. "Try to believe me. I'm a nuclear physicist. At least, I was in 1944."

"I don't understand," said the priest.

"I worked in a secret fission plant deep in the Rocky Mountains."

"In the Rocky Mountains?"

"No one ever heard of it," said the prisoner. "It was never publicized. It was built in 1943 for experiments on nuclear fission."

"But Oak Ridge . . ."

"That was another one. It was strictly a limited venture. Mostly guesswork. Only a few people outside of the plant knew anything about it."

"But . . ."

"Listen. We were working with U-238."

The priest started to speak.

"That's an isotope of uranium. Constitutes the bulk of it; more than 99 percent. But there was no way to make it undergo fission. We were trying to make it do that. Do you understand . . ."

The priest's face reflected his confusion.

"Never mind," said the prisoner hurriedly. "It doesn't matter. What matters is that there was an explosion."

"An . . ."

"An explosion, an explosion."

"Oh. But . . ." faltered the priest.

"This was in 1944," said the prisoner. "That's . . . ten years ago. Now I wake up and I'm here in . . . where are we?"

"State Penitentiary," prompted the priest without thinking.

"Colorado?"

The priest shook his head.

"This is New York," he said.

The prisoner's left hand rose to his forehead. He ran nervous fingers through his hair.

"Two thousand miles," he muttered. "Ten years."

"My son . . ."

He looked at the priest.

"Don't you believe me?"

The priest smiled sadly. The prisoner gestured helplessly with his hands.

"What can I do to prove it? I know it sounds fantastic. Blown through time and space."

He knitted his brow.

"Maybe I didn't get blown through time and space. Maybe I was blown out of my mind. Maybe I became someone else. Maybe . . ."

"Listen to me, Riley."

The prisoner's face contorted angrily.

"I told you. I'm *not* Riley."

The priest lowered his head.

"Must you do this thing?" he asked. "Must you try so hard to escape justice?"

"Justice?" cried the prisoner. "For God's sake is this justice? I'm no criminal. I'm not even the man you say I am."

"Maybe we'd better pray together," said the priest.

The prisoner looked around desperately. He leaned forward and grasped the priest's shoulders.

"Don't . . ." started Father Shane.

"I'm not going to hurt you," said the prisoner impatiently. "Just tell me about this Riley. Who is he? All right, all right," he went on as the priest gave him an imploring look. "Who am I supposed to be? What's my background?"

"My son, why must you . . ."

"Will you *tell* me. For God's sake I'm to be exec— . . . that's it isn't it? Isn't it?"

The priest nodded involuntarily.

"In less than two hours. Won't you do what I ask?"

The priest sighed.

"What's my education?" asked the prisoner.

"I don't know," said Father Shane. "I don't know your education, your background, your family, or . . ."

"But it's not likely that John Riley would know nuclear physics is it?" inquired the prisoner anxiously. "Not likely is it?"

The priest shrugged slightly.

"I suppose not," he said.

"What did he . . . what did I do?"

The priest closed his eyes.

"Please," he said.

"What did I do?"

The priest clenched his teeth.

"You stole," he said. "You murdered."

The prisoner looked at him in astonishment. His throat contracted. Without realizing it, he clasped his hands together until the blood drained from them.

"Well," he mumbled, "if I . . . if he did these things, it's not likely he's an educated nuclear physicist is it?"

"Riley, I . . ."

"*Is* it!"

"No. No, I suppose not. What's the purpose of asking?"

"I *told* you. I can give you facts about nuclear physics. I can tell you things that you admit this Riley could never tell you."

The priest took a troubled breath.

"Look," the prisoner hurriedly explained. "Our trouble stemmed from the disparity between theory and fact. In theory the U-238 would capture a neutron and form a new isotope U-239 since the neutron would merely add to the mass of . . ."

"My son, this is useless."

"Useless!" cried the prisoner. "Why? *Why?* You tell me Riley couldn't know these things. Well, I know them. Can't you see that it means I'm not Riley. And if I became Riley, it was because of loss of memory. It was due to an explosion ten years ago that I had no control over."

Father Shane looked grim. He shook his head.

"That's right isn't it?" pleaded the prisoner.

"You may have read these things somewhere," said the priest. "You may have just remembered them in this time of stress. Believe me I'm not accusing you of . . ."

"I've told the truth!"

"You must struggle against this unmanly cowardice," said Father Shane. "Do you think I can't understand your fear of death? It is universal. It is . . ."

"Oh God, is it possible," moaned the prisoner. "Is it possible?"

The priest lowered his head.

"They can't execute me!" the prisoner said, clutching at the priest's dark coat. "I tell you I'm not Riley. I'm Phillip Johnson."

The priest said nothing. He made no resistance. His body jerked in the prisoner's grip. He prayed.

The prisoner let go and fell back against the wall with a thud.

"My God," he muttered. "Oh, my God, is there no one?"

The priest looked up at him.

"There is God," he said. "Let Him take you to His bosom. Pray for forgiveness."

The prisoner stared blankly at him.

"You don't understand," he said in a flat voice. "You just don't understand. I'm going to be executed."

His lips began to tremble.

"You don't believe me," he said. "You think I'm lying. Everyone thinks I'm lying."

Suddenly he looked up.

"Mary!" he cried. "My wife. What about my wife?"

"You have no wife, Riley."

"No wife? Are you telling me I have no wife?"

"There's no point in continuing this, my son."

The prisoner reached up despairing hands and drove them against his temples.

"My God, isn't there anyone to listen?"

"Yes," murmured the priest.

Footsteps again. There was loud grumbling from the other prisoners.

Charlie appeared.

"You better go, Father," he said. "It's no use. He don't want your help."

"I hate to leave the poor soul in this condition."

The prisoner jumped up and ran to the barred door. Charlie stepped back.

"Watch out," he threatened.

"Listen, will you call my wife?" begged the prisoner. "Will you? Our home is in Missouri, in St. Louis. The number is . . ."

"Knock it off."

"You don't understand. My wife can explain everything. She can tell you who I really am."

Charlie grinned.

"By God, this is the best I ever seen," he said appreciatively.

"Will you call her?" said the prisoner.

"Go on. Get back in your cell."

The prisoner backed away. Charlie signaled and the door slid open. Father Shane went out, head lowered.

"I'll come back," he said.

"Won't you call my wife?" begged the prisoner.

The priest hesitated. Then, with a sigh, he stopped and took out a pad and pencil.

"What's the number?" he asked wearily.

The prisoner scuttled to the door.

"Don't waste your good time, Father," Charlie said.

The prisoner hurriedly told Father Shane the number.

"Are you sure you have it right?" he asked the priest. "Are you positive?" He repeated the number. The priest nodded.

"Tell her I . . . tell her I'm all right. Tell her I'm well and I'll be home as soon as . . . hurry! There isn't time. Get word to the governor or somebody."

The priest put his hand on the man's shaking shoulder.

"If there's no answer when I call," he said. "If no one is there, then will you stop this talk?"

"There will be. She'll be there. I know she'll be there."

"If she isn't."

"She will be."

The priest drew back his hand and walked down the corridor slowly, nodding at the other prisoners as he passed them. The prisoner watched him as long as he could.

Then he turned back. Charlie was grinning at him.

"You're the best one yet, all right," said Charlie.

The prisoner looked at him.

"Once there was a guy," recalled Charlie. "Said he ate a bomb. Said he'd blow the place sky high if we electrocuted him."

He chuckled at the recollection.

"We X-rayed him. He didn't swallow nothing. Except electricity later."

The prisoner turned away and went back to his bunk. He sank down on it.

"There was another one," said Charlie, raising his voice so the others could hear him. "Said he was Christ. Said he couldn't be killed. Said he'd get up in three days and come walkin', through the wall."

He rubbed his nose with a bunched fist.

"Ain't heard from him since," he snickered. "But I always keep an eye on the wall just in case."

His chest throbbed with rumbling laughter.

"Now there was another one," he started. The prisoner looked at him with hate burning in his eyes. Charlie shrugged his shoulders and started back up the corridor. Then he turned and went back.

"We'll be giving you a haircut soon," he called in. "Any special way you'd like it?"

"Go away."

"Sideburns, maybe?" Charlie said, his fat face wrinkling in amusement. The prisoner turned his head and looked at the window.

"How about bangs?" asked Charlie. He laughed and turned back down the wall.

"Hey Mac, how about we give big boy some bangs?"

The prisoner bent over and pressed shaking palms over his eyes.

The door was opening.

The prisoner shuddered and his head snapped up from the bunk. He stared dumbly at Mac and Charlie and the third man. The third man was carrying something in his hand.

"What do you want?" he asked thickly.

Charlie snickered.

"Man, this is rich," he said. "What do we want?"

His face shifted into a cruel leer. "We come to give you a haircut, big boy."

"Where's the priest?"

"Out priesting," said Charlie.

"Shut up," Mac said irritably.

"I hope you're going to take this easy son," said the third man.

The skin tightened on the prisoner's skull. He backed against the wall. "Wait a minute," he said fearfully. "You have the wrong man."

Charlie sputtered with laughter and reached down to grab him. The prisoner pulled back.

"No!" he cried. "Where's the priest?"

"Come *on*," snapped Charlie angrily.

The prisoner's eyes flew from Mac to the third man.

"You don't understand," he said hysterically. "The priest is calling my wife in St. Louis. She'll tell you all who I am. I'm not Riley. I'm Phillip Johnson."

"Come on, Riley," said Mac.

"Johnson, Johnson!"

"Johnson, Johnson come and get your hair cut Johnson, Johnson," chanted Charlie, grabbing the prisoner's arm.

"Let go of me!"

Charlie jerked him to his feet and twisted his arm around. His face was taut with vicious anger.

"Grab him," he snapped to Mac. Mac took hold of the prisoner's other arm.

"For God's sake, what do I have to do!" screamed the prisoner, writhing in their grip. "I'm not Johnson. I mean I'm not Riley."

"We heard you the first time," panted Charlie. "Come on. Shave him!"

They slammed the prisoner down on the bunk and twisted his arms behind him. He screamed until Charlie back-handed him across the mouth.

"Shut up!"

The prisoner sat trembling while his hair fluttered to the floor in dark heaps. Tufts of hair stuck to his eyebrows. A trickle of blood ran from the edge of his mouth. His eyes were stricken with horror.

When the third man had finished on the prisoner's head, he bent down and slashed open his pants.

"Mmmm," he grunted. "Burned legs."

The prisoner jerked down his head and looked. His mouth formed soundless words. Then he cried out.

"Flash burns! Can you see them? They're from an atomic explosion. Now will you believe me?"

Charlie grinned. They let go of the prisoner and he fell down on the bunk. He pushed up quickly and clutched at Mac's arm.

"You're intelligent," he said. "Look at my legs. Can't you see that they're flash burns?"

Mac picked the prisoner's fingers off his arm.

"Take it easy," he said.

The prisoner moved toward the third man.

"You saw them," he pleaded. "Don't you know a flash burn? Look. L-look. Take my word for it. It's a flash burn. No other kind of heat could make such scars. *Look at it!*"

"Sure, sure, sure," said Charlie moving into the corridor. "We'll take your word for it. We'll get your clothes and you can go right home to your wife in Saint Louie."

"I'm telling you they're flash burns!"

The three men were out of the cell. They slid the door shut. The prisoner reached through the bars and tried to stop them. Charlie punched his arm and shoved him back. The prisoner sprawled onto the bunk.

"For God's sake," he sobbed, his face twisted with childish frenzy. "What's the matter with you? Why don't you listen to me?"

He heard the men talking as they went down the corridor. He wept in the silence of his cell.

After a while the priest came back. The prisoner looked up and saw him standing at the door. He stood up and ran to the door. He clutched at the priest's arm.

"You reached her? You reached her?"

The priest didn't say anything.

"You did, didn't you?"

"There was no one there by that name."

"What?"

"There was no wife of Phillip Johnson there. Now will you listen to me?"

"Then she moved. Of course! She left the city after I . . . after the explosion. You have to find her."

"There's no such person."

The prisoner stared at him in disbelief.

"But I told you . . ."

"I'm speaking truth. You're making it all up in a vain hope to cheat . . ."

"I'm not making it up! For God's sake listen to me. Can't you . . . wait, wait."

He held his right leg up.

"Look," he said eagerly, "These are flash burns. From an atomic explosion. Don't you see what that means?"

"Listen to me, my son."

"Don't you understand?"

"Will you listen to me?"

"Yes but . . ."

"Even if what you say is true . . ."

"It *is* true."

"Even if it is. You still committed the crimes you're here to pay for."

"But it wasn't me!"

"Can you prove it?" asked the priest.

"I . . . I . . ." faltered the prisoner. "These legs . . ."

"They're no proof."

"My wife . . ."

"Where is she?"

"I don't know. But you can find her. She'll tell you. She can save me."

"I'm afraid there's nothing that can be done."

"But there has to be! Can't you look for my wife. Can't you get a stay of execution while you look for her? Look, I have friends, a lot of them. I'll give you all their addresses. I'll give you names of people who work for the government who . . ."

"What would I say, Riley?" interrupted the priest sharply.

"Johnson!"

"Whatever you wish to be called. What would I say to these people? I'm calling about a man who was in an explosion ten years ago? But he didn't die? He was blown into . . ."

He stopped.

"Can't you see?" he entreated. "You must face this. You're only making it more difficult for yourself."

"But . . ."

"Shall I come in and pray for you?"

The prisoner stared at him. Then the tautness sapped from his face and stance. He slumped visibly. He turned and staggered back to his bunk and fell down on it. He leaned against the wall and clutched his shirtfront with dead curled fingers.

"No hope," he said. "There's no hope. No one will believe me. No one."

He was lying down on his bunk when the other two guards came. He was staring, glassy-eyed, at the wall. The priest was sitting on the stool and praying.

The prisoner didn't speak as they led him down the corridor. Only once he raised his head and looked around as though all the world was a strange incomprehensible cruelty.

Then he lowered his head and shuffled mutely between the guards. The priest followed, hands folded, head lowered, his lips moving in silent prayer.

Later, when Mac and Charlie were playing cards the lights went out. They sat there waiting. They heard the other prisoners in death row stirring restlessly.

Then the lights went on.

"You deal," said Charlie.

Always Before Your Voice

M R. SMALLEY MOVED TO VERA BEACH on Wednesday, March seventeenth. The morning of that day Miss Land was distributing the 11:30 delivery when he came in. She heard the doorbell tinkle and the squeak of the floor-boards as he crossed over to the stamp and postal order window. She finished slipping the *Brook County Newsletter* into the boxes and turned.

Through the tarnished window bars she saw a tall, dark-haired man wearing a brown leather jacket. He looked in his early thirties.

"Hello," he said, smiling. "I just moved here. I'd like to rent a box if I could." His voice was mild and deeply-pitched.

"I'm sorry," Miss Land told him. "I'm afraid all the boxes are taken."

"Oh." The man's smile faded. "And I suppose there's only one house delivery a day."

"We don't deliver to the houses," said Miss Land. "You'll have to have your mail sent in care of general delivery."

"Oh. I see." The man nodded, looking a little perturbed. "And—how many deliveries are there a day?"

Miss Land told him.

"I see. Well . . ."

"If you'd like to put your name on the waiting list for boxes," Miss Land said.

"Yes. I would," he said.

After he'd written down his name and said that yes, he'd given his previous post office a change of address card, the tall man left. Miss Land stood at the stamp window watching him walk across the wind-scoured square to a black Volkswagen. She watched him get in and her right hand fingered unconsciously at the gold locket around her neck.

When the man had driven away, she blinked her eyes and turned away from the window. "Hi ho," she murmured. She walked slowly over to her desk, looking at the name he'd written on the list. *Louis Smalley.*

That's a nice name, Miss Land thought. She wondered if Mr. Smalley had brought his family to Vera Beach with him.

Just before one o'clock, Miss Land's mother phoned and told her to bring some lemons and sugar from the store when she came home for lunch.

Every morning when she'd finished sorting and distributing the seven o'clock delivery, Miss Land walked across the square to Meldick's Candy Store for a cup of coffee and a cruller. By nine-fifteen she was back at the post office.

The morning after Mr. Smalley had moved to Vera Beach, Miss Land found him waiting at the closed general delivery window when she got back.

"Morning," he said.

She smiled and nodded and let herself in through the back door. She took off her coat and put down her handbag. Her hands moved over her pale, brown hair, they ran smoothingly over her dark dress. Then she let up the window.

"That was Smalley, wasn't it?" she asked.

The tall man nodded. "That's right," he said.

She drew out a small packet of envelopes from the *S* shelf and fingered through them.

"No, nothing today," she said.

Mr. Smalley nodded. "Well, it's a little too soon yet," he said and left.

Miss Land stood at the window watching him walk across the square to his Volkswagen. That's a funny car, she thought. She watched him pull open the door and duck in, then she turned away. *Mr. Smalley*. The name was spoken once in her mind.

Later she found the letters and cards he'd put in the box under the stamp window. She picked them up and looked at them. They were all neatly typed. She held them in her hands a moment, then walked over to the mail sack and dropped them in.

Ten minutes later she drew them out again, thinking that she ought to see if Mr. Smalley had put down the correct return address. She swallowed dryly as she held them in her hands.

There were three letters and a postcard. She saw that the return address was correct on all of them. She looked at the letters. Two of them were going to New York City, the third to Los Angeles. The postcard was addressed to New Jersey.

Miss Land turned the card over.

Dear Harry, it read. *Trying the Island on for size. Address is General Delivery, Vera Beach, N. Y. Any word yet from Heller about MIDNIGHT DRUM? Am working on a few shorts before starting the novel for Cappington. Okay? Best to all. Lou.*

Nervously, Miss Land dropped the letters and the post-card back into the mail sack. I shouldn't have read it, she thought as she went over to her desk. She started checking the previous day's postal money order receipts.

The next morning Mr. Smalley was waiting again.

"I'm sorry," said Miss Land and she explained to him about the coffee break.

"Oh, that's all right," said Mr. Smalley. "If I'd known I'd have joined you in a cup."

Miss Land took off her coat hastily in back. She felt at her curls automatically and adjusted her dress, then drew up the general delivery window. There were two letters for Mr. Smalley forwarded from Manhattan. Mr. Smalley said, "Oh, good."

"Cold for this time of the year," Miss Land said as he was looking at the envelopes.

Mr. Smalley looked up with a smile.

"Certainly is," he said. "Especially when you're used to California weather."

"Oh, is that where you're from?" Miss Land's gaze held a moment on his face.

He told her he'd decided to move east to see if he'd like it.

"Well, I hope you'll like it here," said Miss Land.

"I think I'll like it very much," said Mr. Smalley.

Miss Land watched him leave. She shivered briefly as a cold wind from the opened door laced across her cheek. She crossed her arms and rubbed at them with her hands. Cold, she thought as she watched Mr. Smalley walk quickly across the square to his car.

She stood there until he'd read the letters and driven away. Then she turned for her desk. Well, I hope you and your family will like it here, her question re-phrased itself in her mind. She would have found out about his wife and children if she'd asked him that.

Miss Land went to her work with great efficiency. What difference, she thought, did that make to her?

It was the following Monday that she found out about Mr. Smalley.

She was having her coffee and cruller at Meldick's when Mr. Cirucci who owned the square grocery store came in.

They said good morning and Mr. Cirucci sat down on the stool beside Miss Land.

"See we got us a celebrity," said Mr. Cirucci after the topics of weather, business and mail had been disposed of.

"Oh?" said Miss Land. The coffee had steamed up her rimless glasses and she was rubbing at the lenses with a fresh Kleenex.

"Mr. Smalley," said Mr. Cirucci. "He's a writer."

"Is that so?" said Miss Land, enjoying the mild illicitness of already knowing.

"Yes ma'am," said Mr. Cirucci. "He writes books. History stories."

"Oh. How nice." Miss Land was mentally watching Mr. Smalley walk across the square to his funny little Volkswagen.

Then the question occurred to her and she legitimized her nervous swallow with a sip of coffee. How could she phrase it?

"Yes, ma'am. He lives over on Brookhaven Road. Rents Miz Salinger's place."

"Oh. Yes," said Miss Land, nodding. That was a small house.

"He—has no children then," she heard herself saying.

"He's not even married," said Mr. Cirucci, not noticing the color in Miss Land's cheeks.

He only heard her say, quite faintly, *"Oh."*

She saw his car turn the corner and her half-full cup clinked down loudly in the stillness of the candy store. Mr. Meldick looked up from his newspaper. He saw Miss Land fumbling in her handbag.

"Somethin' wrong?" he asked.

"No, I just have so much work to do," Miss Land said. "I really shouldn't have snuck out this morning. It's a bad habit, I know, but then—"

She cut herself short and put two dimes on the counter for the coffee and untouched cruller. She turned away before Mr. Meldick could see the flush across her cheeks.

"Bye now," said Mr. Meldick.

"Good—" Miss Land cleared her throat hastily. "Goodbye Mr. Meldick," she said as she started for the door.

Cold wind whipped the hem of her coat around her thin legs as she hurried across the square. She made the post office just as Mr. Smalley came walking up.

"Tie," said Mr. Smalley.

Miss Land smiled nervously, then nodded as he opened the door for her.

"Certainly is cold," she said.

"North Polish," he answered. She didn't hear exactly what he'd said but she smiled anyway.

When she drew up the general delivery window her windblown hair was back in place.

"Well, now," she said and she drew out the packet of letters from the *S* shelf.

"I don't believe I know your name," said Mr. Smalley.

"Miss Land," she said as she looked through the letters. She was pleased at how casual she sounded.

"Miss Land," he repeated.

Two letters slipped from her fingers and fluttered palely to the floor. "Oh, dear," she murmured, hoping that her face felt warm because of the oil stove's buffeting heat. She bent down quickly and picked up the letters.

"There," she said, putting his mail on the counter.

"Well," he said, "I really hit the jackpot today."

"You certainly did," she said, smiling.

He smiled back at her and turned away. She stood there watching him walk across the square, examining his mail. When he'd driven away she got a Kleenex from her handbag and patted at the dew of sweat across her forehead. The jackpot, she thought with a smile.

He was a writer, all right.

He corresponded with writers in Los Angeles, New York City, Milwaukee, Phoenix and his agent in New Jersey. He subscribed to *The Saturday Review*, *The National Geographic Magazine*, *The New Yorker* and *The Manchester Guardian*. He was a member of the Book Find Club. He typed all his mail and sent most of it in envelopes except for an occasional postcard. As far as could be judged by handwriting and return addresses he received no letters from women.

This Miss Land had discovered in several weeks of observation.

She sat at her desk looking at the wall clock. It was nine-thirty and Mr. Smalley was late. Miss Land fingered at the magazine on her desk. It had been forwarded from Los Angeles. There was three cents due on it. That meant she would have a few moments talk with Mr. Smalley.

She was stroking the magazine distractedly when the doorbell tinkled. Her fingers jerked away and she stood up quickly, smiling.

Mrs. Barbara sent a package to her brother in Naples.

Mr. Smalley didn't come in all that day. Miss Land kept the office open an extra half hour because she had some special work to finish up. Then her mother phoned and Miss Land went home to a restless evening.

"I was wondering what happened to you," she said impulsively when Mr. Smalley came in the next morning.

"Oh." He smiled. "I had to drive into the city," he said.

"Oh." She handed him his mail. "There's three cents due on this," she said.

"Okay." He fumbled in the right-hand pocket of his trousers.

"Have you given your change of address to them?" Miss Land asked, looking at the dark tangle of hair as he picked at the mound of change in his palm.

His eyes met hers. "Yes, I did," he said. "I guess I'd better send them another notice."

"It might be a good idea," said Miss Land.

After Mr. Smalley was gone she sat at her desk staring at the clock. After a few minutes she became conscious of the fact that she was trembling and she pressed her thin lips together and looked angry.

I must be getting a chill, Miss Land said to herself and proceeded to identify herself with her work.

*

On Wednesday it poured. Mr. Smalley didn't get in until almost one. Miss Land was deliberating whether she should have her lunch in the candy store instead of getting soaked walking home when Mr. Smalley came in, his hat and raincoat darkly wet.

"You're late," said Miss Land, her hands unconsciously smoothing at the skirt of her dress.

"Couldn't get my darn car started," he said. "No garage where I am."

"Oh," she said. She gave him his mail. "Don't catch cold now," she said. Her heartbeat jumped she was so startled at her own forwardness.

"I won't, Miss Land." He looked up from his letters. "That's a nice dress," he said and left.

Miss Land stood watching his tall form run across the rain-swept square. Once he slipped and almost fell and Miss Land gasped, a sudden constriction binding her chest. Mr. Smalley righted himself and made the car safely.

"You'd better be more careful there, my lad," Miss Land said lightly to herself.

She shuddered a little. *No*, she thought. It was all she allowed herself. She got her coat and umbrella and started out, then went back and phoned her mother and said it was raining too hard, she was going to have lunch at Mr. Meldick's candy store.

Which was empty. Miss Land carried her bowl of tomato soup, her chopped egg on wheat bread sandwich and her cup of coffee to one of the wooden booths.

She sat there eating slowly, listening to the drumming of rain on the roof, the splattering of it outside the door. The soup tasted delicious as it trickled warmly down her throat. The sandwich was also delicious. Miss Land kept looking down at her dress.

When she'd finished eating, she sat running one finger around the smooth warm lip of the empty cup. I love coffee,

I love tea, the rhyme appeared. She blinked away the remainder of it and took in a deep breath. She looked around the dimly lit candy store. It was peaceful, she thought, very peaceful here in Vera Beach.

She looked at the jukebox a long time and glanced at Mr. Meldick a long time before she struggled out of the booth and walked toward it.

"Somethin'?" Mr. Meldick asked, looking up.

"Just thought I'd have a little music," she replied.

She stood in front of the jukebox's Technicolor bubbling and looked at the titles. There were a lot of love songs. She put a nickel in and the little green SELECT light went on. A little cheerful music, she thought, something relaxing. Her finger wavered over the buttons, then, abruptly, pushed one in.

Before she'd reached the booth the music started.

"If I loved you," sang the woman, *"Time and again I would try to say."*

Miss Land sat looking at her hands on the table, glancing at Mr. Meldick. When she saw that he wasn't paying attention to anything but his *Herald-Tribune* crossword puzzle she relaxed. She leaned her heart back against the booth and closed her eyes. Warm breath trickled out between her lips.

The woman sang, *"Wanting to tell you but afraid and shy."*

The next day Mr. Smalley didn't speak or smile and when Miss Land dropped one of his letters she heard him tap his fingers impatiently on the window counter. When she handed him his mail he turned immediately and left without a word.

Miss Land stood motionless watching him walk across the square. Even after he'd driven away she stared at the place where his car had been, a look of hurt confusion on her face.

She began to recount the sequence of actions between his entrance and his exit. She went over every step, watching herself as she smiled and said good morning and got his mail and handed it to him. Was it because she'd dropped one of his letters? But he'd looked glum from the moment he'd entered.

At five-thirty when she locked up the office she still didn't understand.

A little after seven she got up from the supper table and went for a walk while her mother did the dishes. She walked for several miles along the dark, windy roads listening to the far-off explosions of the surf. She looked at every street sign when she passed it even though she knew that Brookhaven Road was far away from there.

At nine o'clock her mother went to bed and Miss Land sat watching television. It was a comedy program but Miss Land saw only veiled sorrow in it and she turned it off.

It was after eleven when she sat up in bed and stared around her small, dark room. She should take a sedative, she thought. Maybe she'd had too much coffee that day. She decided it was that.

She turned on the table lamp and sat on the edge of the bed, her feet resting in a pool of light. She turned on the radio very softly and listened to Andre Kostelanetz's orchestra playing "Lotus Land." She stared down at her white kneecaps and at the pale curl of her toes on the rug. There were veins like blue cords in her ankles. She thought—In a month and a day I'll be thirty-seven.

She took the book off her bedside table and opened it. It was a Modern Library anthology of poetry she'd bought one day on a trip to the city. Her eyes moved idly down the index of first lines near the back of the book until she came to a particular line. Then she turned to page 875. The poem was written by e.e. cummings.

Always before your voice my soul
half beautiful and wholly droll
is as some smooth and awkward foal

She read the entire poem twice and read aloud the lines:

"But my heart smote in trembling thirds
of anguish quivers to your words
as a—"

"Jessica?"

The book thumped shut loudly. Miss Land looked up and saw her mother standing in the hallway like a bulky ghost, her head alive with curlers.

"Are you sick?" her mother asked.

"No, Mother. Go back to bed."

"You've been drinking too much coffee again," said her mother.

"I'm all right, Mother," said Miss Land.

"You shouldn't drink so much coffee," said her mother. "I always said that."

"Yes, Mother."

Later, lying in the warm center of her bed, Miss Land stared at the ceiling, her shallow chest almost still. There was a tight pain around her heart. Gas, she thought.

Suddenly, with a grunt, she brushed at something crawling down her cheek. And when she discovered it wasn't an insect she rubbed her wet fingers against the spread until the tips felt warm. This is *nonsense!* she told herself.

The next morning Mr. Smalley smiled at her. Miss Land felt very sleepy around noon and took a refreshing nap during her lunch hour.

It was May and Mr. Smalley had dropped a postcard into the box under the stamp and postal order window. Miss Land had it in front of her on the desk. Her heartbeat staggered as she read it again.

Dear Sir: I am interested in the possibilities of renting a small house in the area around Port Jervis. Would you let me know what you have available? Louis Smalley.

Once when Miss Land was seven her dog had been crushed by a truck. She felt the same way now. That identical sense of frozen disbelief. That almost angry conviction that there was no place in life for such an occurrence.

Five times that day Miss Land took the postcard out of the sack and read it. At last she dropped it for the last time and watched it flutter down onto the pile of mail.

Tuesday nights she and her mother usually went to the movies in Port Franklin but that night Miss Land told her mother she had a nagging headache and went to bed early. Her mother stayed home and watched television instead. Miss Land could hear the programs from her room as she lay there in the darkness, her pale blue eyes staring at the ceiling.

At ten-seventeen p.m. her lips pressed together. So Vera Beach wasn't good enough for him. Well, that was just too bad. Miss Land turned over and beat her pillow into submission.

Later, in the very still of night, she bit the pillow till her jaws ached and her body shuddered on the bed. I *hate* him! someone screamed.

When the doorbell tinkled in the morning Miss Land glanced over her shoulder, then went back to sorting.

Mr. Smalley said nothing for a moment. She stood there sliding letters into their proper shelves.

"Anything for Smalley?" he finally asked.

"I'll be finished in a moment," said Miss Land.

She heard him exhale slowly. She picked up another bundle of letters she just hadn't had time to get to that morning.

"Can you tell me if there's anything?" asked Mr. Smalley.

"I really don't know," she said. "I'll be finished in a moment." She felt a cold, drawing sensation in her stomach. Her throat was dry.

Finally she was done.

"Smalley," she said and pulled out the packet of mail on the *S* shelf. She looked through them slowly.

"No, nothing today, Mr. Smalley," she said.

She felt his eyes hold on her an extra moment before he turned and left. She shuddered once as she watched him cross the square. There!—she thought suddenly. *There!* She drew in a quick breath and went over to her desk. She sat there with her eyes shut, hands trembling in her lap.

The next morning she glanced over from her desk and said, "No, nothing."

The next morning she came back late from having coffee and found him waiting at the door. When she handed him the magazine with postage due she said, curtly, "I think you'd better tell them your new address again."

The next morning she handed him his mail without a word and turned away.

On Monday she said lightly, *"Nothing,"* and she didn't even turn to look at him.

That night she got severe stomach cramps and had to stay in bed for three days and nights. She phoned the office once each day to remind her replacement to be very sure she collected on all postage due items. Like things that were forwarded from other cities. Like Los Angeles for instance.

When the letter in the blue envelope arrived Miss Land only glanced at it before sliding it onto the *S* shelf.

Later, when she returned from Meldick's she drew the letter out again. Even if there were no return address on it she could have told from the delicate curve of the handwriting. As it was the name printed on the flap was Marjorie Kelton.

Miss Land sat at her desk holding the letter in her hands. She could feel her heart beating in heavy labored pulsings that seemed to strike the wall of her chest. Marjorie Kelton. She read the name over and over, the letters dark blue on blue. She read it until the letters blurred. Marjorie Kelton. Personal stationery. The air seemed close. Miss Land seemed to feel the chair rocking slowly under her. Her head felt numb. Marjorie Kelton's personal stationery. Miniature pearls of sweat hung from Miss Land's brow. Marjorie Kelton.

When the doorbell tinkled and Mr. Smalley appeared at the general delivery window Miss Land said, "Nothing."

Aghast, she twitched on the chair. She began to cry, "Wait!" but only made a faintly hollow sound in her throat. The doorbell tinkled again. Miss Land raked back her chair and hurried to the window.

"*Wait*," she said.

She watched him walking brusquely to his car.

"I made a mistake," she said. Mr. Smalley got into his car and drove away without answering.

Miss Land turned from the window with a shudder. I made a mistake, she repeated in her mind. A mistake, you see. I didn't put your letter on the right shelf.

A stage smile drew artificially at her thin features. She laughed as she related to Mr. Smalley the humorous incident. I put it on the M shelf, you see. I guess I just wasn't thinking. Wasn't that silly?

The scene dissolved. Miss Land had the phone in her hand. She dropped it back on its cradle. No, not so soon. That would be suspicious. Her eyes fluttered up to the wall clock. In an hour. An hour would be appropriate. Mr. Meldick came in for his mail you see and I ran across your letter. I'd put it on the M shelf by mistake. Wasn't that—

She went about her work.

At ten-thirty she looked through the telephone directory

and a terrible cold stone lay on her stomach when she saw that Mr. Smalley's name wasn't listed.

"*Oh.*" Miss Land shook her head in self-reproachment. Mr. Smalley had just moved in. How *could* he be listed?

But what if he had no phone? Terror scraped at Miss Land's heart. Hastily, she laughed it away. Oh, for heaven's sake, why wasn't she thinking? Mr. Smalley would be in around noon for his second delivery. She'd give him the letter then. That was all.

Mr. Smalley didn't come in again that day. At two o'clock Miss Land called information and requested the number of his newly installed phone.

She sat there five minutes listening to the buzz-click of his unanswered line. Then, almost soundlessly, she slipped the receiver back in place and stared at the blue letter on her desk. Well, it's not my fault, she thought. Well, what am I worrying about? she thought. Mr. Smalley would get it tomorrow.

Tomorrow.

"You haven't eaten a *thing*," her mother said, threatening with a spoonful of mashed potato.

"I'm not *hungry*, Mother," said Miss Land.

"You had something in Meldick's this afternoon," said her mother.

"No, Mother. Please. I'm just not hungry."

Her mother grunted. Then there was the sound of her mother's fork clicking from dinner plate to dental plate, the sound of water being swallowed, the wheezing breath that passed her mother's nostrils. Miss Land drew tiny roads through her untouched mound of potato. She stared at the plate and there was a sharp gnawing at her stomach.

"Finish the meat," her mother said.

"I'm—" Miss Land cleared her throat. "I told you I'm not hungry, Mother."

"You've been drinking too much coffee," said her mother. "It stunts the appetite. I always said it."

"Excuse me, Mother," said Miss Land, getting up.

"You haven't eaten a *thing*," her mother said as Miss Land left the room.

Quietly, she locked her door and went over to her bed. She sat there kneading white fingers together, trying to catch her breath. Every time she drew in air it seemed to drain from her instantly.

Five minutes. Abruptly, Miss Land slid her hand under the pillow and drew out the blue envelope.

She turned it over and over as if it had endless sides and she must find the right one. The woman's name flared in her mind and disappeared, it flared and disappeared like an automatic sign. She looked at his name and his address written in Marjorie Kelton's exact feminine hand. She visualized her sitting at her desk and writing down that name: *Mr. Louis Smalley*, surely and casually in the quiet of her room.

Suddenly she tore the envelope open and thought her heart had stopped. The letter fell from her hands and Miss Land sat there trembling, staring down at it, her body rocked with giant heartbeats. She dug her teeth into her lower lip and began to cry softly. It was an accident, her mind fled through the explanation. I thought it was for me, you see, and—

Her eyes pressed shut and she felt two warm tears run down her face. He would never believe that.

"No," she whimpered. "No, no, no."

In a little while she picked the letter up and read it, her face set stiffly, a mask of regal justification.

Lou, Darling! I just heard from Chuck that you were back east! Why in God's name didn't you phone? You know I never meant what I said. Never meant it for a second, damn your luscious bones!

It went on like that. Miss Land sat woodenly, a dull heat licking up through her body as she read. Twice she crumpled up the letter and flung it away and twice retrieved it, pressing out the wrinkles with her fingers. She read it seven times completely and then in sections.

Later in the darkness she lay, holding the crumpled letter in her hand and staring, dry-eyed, at the ceiling, breath a faltering trickle from her lips. She watched Marjorie Kelton and Marjorie Kelton was beautiful and desirable. Miss Land's lips pressed together. Any woman who would write a letter like that . . .

Around midnight Miss Land sat up and slapped around in rabid fury until she'd found the letter and then she tore it up with savage jerkings of her arms and flung the ragged shards into the darkness with a choking sob. *There!*

In the morning she burned the pieces. Mr. Smalley got two letters and a postcard and when Miss Land handed them to him he smiled and said thank you. It doesn't matter, Miss Land decided at lunch. It was only one letter and anything could have happened to it. That was the end of it. She certainly wasn't going to make a fool of herself again.

The following Monday morning the letter from the upstate realtor came for Mr. Smalley and Miss Land put it in her desk drawer. When Mr. Smalley came in she gave him his *Saturday Review* and his notice from the Book Find Club. What amazed her the most was the absence of fright she felt. On the contrary there was a feeling of rich satisfaction in her as she put the letter in her handbag and took it home at lunchtime.

After lunch she retired to her room and, after locking the door, took the letter from her bag. For a long time she lay quietly, touching the envelope, rubbing it experimentally between her fingertips, pressing it against her cheek. Once, suddenly, she kissed it and felt a strange hot pouring sensation in her like a sun-baked river. It made her shiver.

It's really, she thought hastily, a delicious conspiracy against Mr. Smalley. It wasn't doing him any harm. After all it was only a letter from a realtor, nothing important. Miss Land writhed her hips a little on the bed and read the letter. There were rentals available. Miss Land shrugged.

"So what?" she murmured and had to giggle over that.

In a few minutes she tore the letter into pieces and held the scraps high above her and laughed softly and contentedly as they filtered through her spread fingers and fluttered down on her like dry snow.

There, she thought. Her teeth clenched together and anger came again. Oh, *there*.

She fell into a sleep so heavy that her mother had to pound on the door for three minutes straight before she heard it.

She took one of Mr. Smalley's *Saturday Reviews* home and put it under her pillow. Now that's all, she told herself. No more. This much was all right because it was nothing important but that was all. After all there was no point to it really. It was just a silly game.

Two days later she took a postcard from a men's shop in Port Franklin. It wasn't very satisfactory. The next day she took a letter from his agent and tore it up without even reading it.

That's all, Miss Land told herself. After all there's no point in going on with such a silly game.

When he wrote to the realtor again Miss Land tore up the letter with her teeth and hands and threw the pieces all over her room.

On the Wednesday morning of June 22nd Miss Land was sorting mail when she heard the door opened. The beginning of a smile twisted playfully on her lips, then was gone. She kept sliding letters and postcards onto the general delivery shelves.

"Pardon me," said an unfamiliar voice.

Miss Land looked over her shoulder and saw a man wearing a dark blue suit and a panama hat. There were palm trees on his tie.

The man pressed his hat brim between two fingers and Miss Land came forward. "Yes?" she said.

The man drew a billfold from his inside coat pocket and opened it. Miss Land looked down at the card he showed her.

"I'd like to talk to you, Miss Land," he said.

"Oh?" she said. Her fingers were rigid on the bundle of mail. "What about?"

"May I come in back?"

"It's against the rules," said Miss Land.

The man held out his card again.

"I know what's against the rules," he said.

Miss Land swallowed once. It made a dry clicking sound in her throat.

"I'm so busy," she said. "I have so much mail to sort."

The man looked at her without any expression on his face.

"The door, Miss Land," he said.

Miss Land put down the bundle of mail on the table. She pushed in at the edges to even them. Then she walked over to the door. The man's footsteps stopped there. Miss Land stood a moment looking through the frosted glass at the dark outline of the man. Then she unlocked the door.

"Come in," she said, cheerfully. "You won't mind if I continue with my work while we talk."

She turned before the man could answer. From the corners of her eyes she saw him walk in, hat in hand, and heard the click as the door was closed again. A shudder laced down her back.

"Well, what is it?" she asked, picking up the mail. "Somebody complaining about me?" Her laugh was faint and hollow. "You can't please all of the people all of the time. Or is it—?"

"I think it would be better if we shut the windows for a while, don't you?" interrupted the man.

"No, that's impossible," said Miss Land with a fleeting smile. "The office is open, you see. People will be coming in for their mail. After all, that's what I'm here for. I can't just close—*just like that*."

She turned back to her bundle of letters and held one up with a shaking hand.

"Mrs. Brandt," she said and slid the letter onto the D shelf.

"Miss Land," started the man.

"*Close* in here, isn't it?" said Miss Land. "I've written the main office about it, oh, dozens of times. I guess I'll just have to get a fan for myself."

The man walked to the stamp and postal order window and pulled it down.

"Now *wait* a minute!" Miss Land said shrilly. "You can't do that. This is a public—"

Her voice broke off as the man looked at her. She stood there frozenly, the bundle of mail held against her chest, as the man went to the other window.

"But you can't do that," said Miss Land. She watched him pull down the general delivery window. A giggle hovered starkly in her throat. "Well," she said, "I guess you did it." She shrugged and held the mail bundle out toward the table.

"*Oh!*" she said as the letters and cards spilled all over the tile floor. She crouched down hastily. "Dear me," she said. "I'm all thumbs to—"

"Let them be, Miss Land," the man said firmly. "We'll pick them up later."

"Oh, that's very nice of—"

Miss Land stopped suddenly, realizing that the "we" he mentioned didn't include her. She straightened up dizzily and knotted her hands together.

"Well," she said, "what is it you want to see me about?"

"I think you already know, Miss Land."

"No," she said, too loudly. "No, I have no idea. I—I haven't been honored with a visit from a p-p—"

Miss Land looked stunned. Her shudder was too visible to hide. She cleared her throat suddenly.

"If it's about—" she started, then broke off again.

"Miss Land, we've been checking on this for almost a month. *Twenty-one* items have been reported undelivered by the party in—"

"Oh, that would be Mr. Smalley," Miss Land blurted. "Oh, he's a strange man. *Strange*, Mr.—"

The man didn't say. Miss Land cleared her throat.

"He's a writer, you know," she said. "You can't—rely on that t-type of man. Why he wasn't here more than two weeks before he started looking for another place to stay because he didn't like—"

"We have the evidence, Miss Land," the man said. "I'd like you to come with me."

"Oh, but—" A terrified smile splashed across her lips. "No, that's impossible. I have people here to serve, you see. You don't understand, you simply don't understand. I have *people* here."

"I have a replacement for you out in my car," said the man.

Miss Land stared at him blankly.

"You—" She ran a shaking hand over her cheek. "But, that's impossible," she said.

"Would you get your things," said the man.

"But a replacement wouldn't know where everything *is*," Miss Land told him cheerfully. "You don't understand. I have my own system here. I call it the—"

She bit her lower lip suddenly and drove back a sob.

"No, no, I'm sorry," she said. "It's impossible. You don't understand. A replacement would never be able to—"

"*Miss Land, get your things.*"

Miss Land was a statue except for the vein that pulsed on her neck.

"But you don't understand," she murmured.

Outside, the doorbell tinkled and Miss Land's head turned. She stared at the general delivery window.

"Miss Land," said the man.

Abruptly, Miss Land stepped over to the general delivery window and jerked it up.

"Well, good *morning*," she said. "Isn't it a lovely morning?"

Mr. Smalley looked at her in blank surprise.

"Well, let's see now," said Miss Land, turning toward the shelves. Her trembling hand drew out the small packet and she put one, two, three, four, five letters on the table. She drew a magazine off the pile, then turned back to the window, smiling and flushed.

"Well," she said. "You certainly hit the jackpot this morning."

She looked right into Mr. Smalley's dark eyes and she held on to the counter edge with bloodless fingers.

When Mr. Smalley had left, she stood watching him for a moment as he walked across the square toward his car. Once he glanced back and she waved to him with a delicate flutter of her fingers.

Then Miss Land drew down the window and turned away from it.

Life Size

THE LITTLER ONE WAS PLAYING with her dollhouse this afternoon. Crinkled knees on rose bespattered rug, she fondled her ones, Molly, Fig and the Puppy Gruff.

Molly is a boy doll. The littler one giggled when I dubbed him so. That is a girl's name, she said. Hush, said I, who is to say?

Fig is a black sambo rajah, jeweled and awesome. And the Puppy Gruff is the Puppy Gruff.

Mother was sitting at the big furniture scraping on a hill of debts.

She frowned at me squatting on a buttoned hassock admiring my daughter.

The littler one was rearranging furniture, a blue-veined hand sliding a bathtub to the wall. You must not place a bathtub in the guestroom, I told her, the guests might float ducks in it. I flew a bit of breeze from my lips and the delicate hair wisps at her temple stirred golden. Pappa, said she with a shake.

The furniture arrangement proved so distasteful that she swept her hand across the floor to brush it clean. The furniture bounced nicely on the rug. I think now, said I, that is some fine way to arrange furniture. Little lips pouting, priceless petulance.

The distaff giant rose, the floor shook with her coming. I looked up and the far off eyes sprinkled ice dust on our heads.

Get up! she cried. I lifted the piano with two fingers. First, I begged, we must return this.

She bent over and slapped it spinning on the floor. Come

here, in a loud way she said. And *you*, a finger spear pointing at my loved one's heart, stay away from the house if you don't appreciate it.

Little head lowered, rising tears. You may play nicely with the house, I said and stood up way high. Mother stamp stamped to the table. I stamp stamped followed.

This simply cannot go on, she gurgled, pushing the everest of bills to me. I am not hungry, I said. Ice dust upon me.

Listen, Reg, she hissed so the littler one would hear worse, this simply is the end. Either you get out and work or I leave, *with* the child.

Old tale. Old song. Old misery set to words. Take *my* child? Nonsense.

I'll get work tomorrow, I promised.

Tomorrow, tomorrow I heard an echo from the valley of her throat. How many times have I heard that? How many times did Sal hear it? Tomorrow I said and walked away. That is not all, she cried but I kept on for the doorway.

It is unbelievable the rapidity with which I shrank.

Suddenly from as big as her, down, down.

Whishhh the doorway far far up like a mountain tunnel. The huge chair noted and prepared to collapse its gargantua crimson on my tiny body. The sky shook, the cliff tottered miles above me.

I flung up my arm and cried fear.

Pain at my knees. Suddenly I was back again, sprawled across the chair. Pappa! sweet worried tones caressed my ears.

Mother had such a look and such a trembling standing by the table.

I rose with dignity and brushed off some dust not on me. I strode into the hall carefully. The house was slowly beginning to rock. The stairs were swelling, receding, in and out, like rolling waves carpeted and tacked.

I held tight to the bannister. No sense being swept out the window and so to sea.

I prisoned off my room and sat down uh! on my white bed. My feet raised up and placed *so* on the spread, I fell back.

The pitching slacked off, my ship slid into calm waters. Oh Sal, I whispered, Sal who understood, Sal not here, Sal far away gone and never coming more.

The clock whispered sleep and wake.

I raised squarely up and was without trouble. The room, the hall, all in fine order, walls square, flat and firm, steady ceiling.

I slid down the silent stairs. Ha ha was the chuckle as I swept past the bottom toe and kneeled before the living room. Murmurs in the kitchen, the way clear. Softly, softly. Hello there Fig old bedizened potentate. Molly.

I began to crawl carefully, slowly.

For a while, naturally, I got nowhere since I kept shrinking the farther I went. The room swelled bigger, bigger. Grotesque universe.

Voices! Footsteps!

I scurried to the brink of the rug meaning to slip quickly over the edge and crouch in a hairy black cavern.

Reg! voice in the distance, crashing from the sky. I could have sworn I was out of sight.

Reg! the thunder roared again.

I wept with fury biting at the roses for their eyes so keen. I raised a look through binocular tears.

The littler one, clever darling, made as though frightened. Sweet conspirator! Mother will not know my plan from her.

I started climbing up the red chair, a long haul without a rope.

Fantastic hands reached down to smother me in hot greasy palms. I clawed at them, angular sweating monstrosities.

The room wavered, so like it to do that.

I stood up, ready to die for my secret, let the black waves dash on me. The room distorted, cooled and shrank. I held up my hands, screaming, ready for the ceiling to plunge down on me.

But first the tower of me crashed an awful way far down on the rug plateau. I saw roses in my eyes when I became unknowing.

I woke in my bed feeling quiet. Someone was sitting across the room.

Come here Sal, I asked so gently. Let me touch your cold grey lips, let me see the clay that stains your eyes.

It was only a white tower that came to me as I slowly drowned in the lake folds of my bed.

Foul lifeguard it reached down and tugged me out. My wrist was enveloped by cold serpents. I heard hmmm at the tower gate. I squinted and saw it was actually a giant whose every pore was a gaping pit.

I turned my head away and was sick it was so ugly and horrible.

I fell away to black things soon.

But before it, I thought this and final too.

When that bleak tower is gone or at slumber I will creep out, fly down the steps of mountain side and run across the rose strewn plain to my home.

In the door, they will leave it open for me. Up, up, up the pretty stairs, two at a time I think.

Into the bed creeping to hear them whisper below, my friends.

Waiting for Sal to tuck me in and kiss me so, *goodnight my dear*. Sleep.

Dream on dream within the smooth and creamy silent walls.

The pendulum stops.

That Was Yesterday

H E ROLLED OVER ON THE BED AND SAT UP. A grunt pressed out from his stomach as he bent over and fumbled for his shoes. He found them after running his fingers over the dusty floor, put them on and tied the laces as if it were the first time.

Then, with a shuddering sigh, he straightened up and stared at the window until the cloud before his eyes lifted. He pushed himself up from the bed and stood, swaying back and forth.

He slid trouser legs over the worn shoes. The ragged tail of his shirt was tucked in. Wrinkled and spattered with hashhouse spots, the coat hung limply on his thin shoulders.

Picking up his cap he plodded to the door and closed it silently behind him. He adjusted the cap as he moved down the hall to the stairs. He went down the insides of the steps so they wouldn't squeak, opened the front door only wide enough to slip through so the hanging bell would not sound out his departure. He looked around carefully before descending the wet porch steps to the sidewalk.

Even though he pulled up his collar, the raindrops rolled under it and down his back. He shuddered, moving closer to the storefronts. The awnings were still rolled up.

He stopped a second to look around. A policeman turned the distant corner and started up the block, head bent into the cold wind.

He scuttled down to an alley and into its murky length. At its end, he clambered over a wooden fence and dropped heavily into a yard piled high with tin cans and refuse. There he crouched down behind a pile of old newspapers and closed his eyes.

The rain soaked through his coat and shirt. It dripped off the end of his nose, into his mouth. The taste of it was foul from the brim of his dirty cap. He pressed both hands under his armpits and bent over, shivering. He fell back, sitting in the muddy grass, and stared vacantly at the drops bouncing off his kneecaps.

It happened so fast it hardly seemed real. Thoughts about it were like dripping wax from a candle, slow and tortured.

A surprise. The young newlywed home early from the office. Pushing open the door with a smile. Sudden fingers pulling the stomach against the backbone. Blind fury.

Her, sprawled out on the couch, white and sordid. The man standing over her and staring openmouthed at the doorway. The horrible shaking of his uncontrollable limbs.

A long black moment. Only yesterday and yet the memory of it is shapeless in a grey void of thought. A scuffle, a scream, something warm spurting across his chest. Crouching against the wall holding a red-bladed knife. A dead man on the floor.

Her, screaming, kneeling beside the man and trying to push her long fingers against the wounds. The knife falling to the floor. Her, burning in horror, clutching at her throat. The blood running down between her breasts, a thin scarlet stream across her white stomach. Her screams again and the sight of her running into the bedroom and slamming the door.

Vague memories of stairs, sidewalks, buildings, passing beneath and above. A city running past to hide him in its depths.

Alone in the dark rented room. The shirt tearing hair from his chest where the blood had dried. Washing. Throwing himself on the bed and finding the quiet pain of sleep. Yesterday.

★

No one came. He straightened up with a groan. He slipped through the mud and, wearily, placed a box against the fence. A splinter ripped open his finger as he slid down the other side. The blood splattered on the wet sidewalk, faded under the cleansing rain.

He wrapped his handkerchief around the torn skin and went back to the street. The policeman was gone.

He crossed over to a small café which sat dimly behind rain streaked windows. He looked in and then entered.

The coffee was set before him. He drizzled sugar into it and stirred. The thin line of warmth ran down his throat and settled comfortingly in his stomach. He drank again and the cup was empty. He asked for a second and drank it as quickly. Then he sat looking at the third cup. It was light brown and creamy with shiny circles floating on top. The light brown of someone's hair. Someone who had lived only in the mind. An impostor under flesh, hiding a blackness under white grace. Would her tomorrows be as barren, her yesterdays as empty?

Only yesterday. Already it seemed a century.

He sipped the coffee and closed his eyes until the drumming on the window stopped. Then he slid off the stool and stood in the doorway looking up and down the street.

Cap pulled down over one eye, he shuffled across to the newsstand and bought the three morning papers. He put them under his coat as he walked slowly, head bent, back to the rooming house.

The bell made no sound as he slid through the doorway. The stairs hardly murmured as he stepped gingerly along the wall. He opened the door to his room quietly and closed it. He turned on the light, threw off his soggy cap and coat and threw himself on the bed. Then he read through the papers.

There was no mention of the crime.

How could that be? There was nothing subtle about it. In the struggle furniture had toppled over. Her screams had run out over the crashing. And she must have called the police.

Maybe it was a trap to make him return. He would not be so foolish.

But this endless waiting. They would probably arrest him sooner or later. Could he bear the endless torture before they found him?

Was it possible she hadn't told the police?

He lay back on the grimy pillow.

What a stupid idea! Hadn't he seen the dirt of her? Didn't he know that her first desire would be for revenge?

He closed his eyes and listened to the methodical clock and the rain, beating again on the window, like tiny waves on a glassy shore.

In the evening he got up before it was dark. He left the house, ate, and bought the two evening newspapers. He read them carefully. There was nothing in them.

There were tears in his eyes as he read. Maybe she didn't tell them. Maybe it was a last gesture.

He twisted his head in rage. No! She was dirty, foul, corrupt. Could he ever forget that vacuous smile, that sensual leer changed to ugly fright at the sight of him?

She had told. No fear of that. And now they were waiting for him. Waiting as a snake waits, in slimy patience, until the bird wanders close enough. Then, the stunning fangs, the slithering body stretching over the corpse.

He ripped all the papers to shreds and threw them on the floor. Then he fell back heavily on the bed, looking at the ceiling. Soon his eyes closed and he dreamt he was swinging over a pit while blood dripped on his eyes from above.

The sunlight in his eyes woke him up. His finger was infected. He pressed out the milky drops and replaced the dirty handkerchief.

No one saw him leave the house. He started up the street finding no beauty in the weather. Breakfast was coffee and doughnuts at the café. Then he bought the morning papers and started back to his room.

Halfway back he saw a policeman coming toward him. The sunlight glinted off the shiny badge and blinded him. The brown club moved in a blur around the policeman's hand.

He stumbled and fell against a store window. His legs would not move, his arms were heavy and dead. The papers slid onto the ground. They knew! He was caught!

He shuddered when the policeman's hand touched him. He opened his eyes and stared.

"Sick, Granpa?" asked the policeman with a smile.

He couldn't speak. He nodded and tried to smile when the policeman handed him the papers and turned away. He stood there, face twitching, watching the policeman walk up the street. He clutched the papers against him.

Then he rushed down the street from shadow to shadow.

Flinging open the door to his room he threw down the papers and fell against the door, closing it. He slid to the floor and read all the papers, mouth hanging open, the breaths shaking his scrawny hands.

There was nothing about it in the paper.

The fools! The idiotic fools!

He lay back against the door and could not keep the blinding tears from his eyes.

Only yesterday. But it seemed so long. Maybe she didn't tell them yet.

It was only yesterday.

Afterword

WRITING AN AFTERWORD TO THIS COLLECTION of my stories will be more a feat of memory than any variety of philosophical analysis.

Let me be frank. These stories—with one exception—were written a long time ago. A *long*, long time ago.

Not that I denounce their age and/or quality. Consequently, some were published in magazines and the one "contemporary" story in Bill Nolan's edited *The Bradbury Chronicles*.

Still, the majority of them were written when I was very young and I have no recollection of where the ideas came from or why I wrote them as I did. One, of course, was an homage to Ray Bradbury. Another was the opening section to a novel on Spiritualism.

When it became apparent that the ultimate manuscript of the novel—an account in detail of each of the three Nielson children—would likely amount to something in the neighborhood of 2,000 pages, I chickened out and never finished it.

I did the same fold on a novel entitled *The Link*. It, too, seemed headed for a 2,000-page length. This time my agent cautioned me that a novel of such bulk would be so costly that readers would be loathe to spend the money. So another multi-thousand pager bit the dust. This one was about all aspects of parapsychology.

I did win one semi-victory on a lengthy novel when Gauntlet Press published *Hunger and Thirst*. I only had to wait half a century to get that one published in a limited edition and that only took place through the thoughtful intervention of my son Richard.

So what am I to do regarding this Afterword to my collection?

Having re-read the stories, I can only comment on them individually with the hope that some glimmer of memory will take me back to the advent of their creation.

RELICS, published in later years by Richard Chizmar in his magazine *Cemetery Dance*, is a story which attempts to spin around the banality of its setting and character behavior to conclude the story with what we writers like to call a "zapper." Hopefully, that zapper has some sociological value. Let the reader decide.

BLUNDER BUSS is one of my not-too-often attempts to write a humorous story. It is a story of a man's sexual fantasy, not at all uncommon in the male gender. And, again, hopefully, the zapper comes—unexpectedly and, even more hopefully, amusingly.

AND NOW I'M WAITING has a history more unique than the other stories.

I wrote it as a dead serious account. When the concept was submitted to *The Twilight Zone* (I don't recall if there was a completed story with it) it was rejected as being, I presume, too grim.

So I turned it into a comedy and titled it "A World of His Own." It starred Keenan Wynn and permitted me to do what no other writer on the series ever did—make my zapper be the literal disappearance of Rod Serling himself.

THE LAST BLAH IN THE ETC. A dread secret revealed. The last page of the manuscript—ancient, of course—had disappeared. I seemed to remember what I had in mind and added two words to the ending to hint at my intention. A trifle enigmatic but a little thought will, I think, reveal the story's denouement.

I have never been in the habit of letting any story's conclusion be in question.

I will be interested to see if you get its point. Maybe everyone will come up with a different one. That would be intriguing.

PHONE CALL FROM ACROSS THE STREET. I don't remember getting the idea but I certainly think its meaning is clear.

It is one of the few stories I wrote in the form of dialogue.

Another was a story published in *The Magazine of Fantasy and Science Fiction* entitled "Through Channels."

Somewhere—undoubtedly in Bill the Collector's vault —sits a recorded (tape) enactment of the story by Bill and myself. I portrayed the boy, Bill played the detective or policeman or whatever authority he was supposed to be.

We recorded it at an evening of what came to be called The California Group. Not bad either. I have always maintained that writers could very well be actors if they wanted to try their hand at it.

Indeed, Bill played a key role in Chuck Beaumont's film *The Intruder*.

And I acted in many plays performed by our community theater, not to mention my two-word role in *Somewhere in Time*.

MAYBE YOU REMEMBER HIM surprised Bill because he had no idea I was a baseball fan.

I was and still am and I wonder why I didn't write more baseball stories. *Hell Stadium? The Shrinking Shortstop? What Hits May Come?*

Just as well I wrote only this one baseball story.

MIRROR MIRROR . . . I have no memory whatsoever of where this story idea came from and when I chose to write it.

I have always fancied the notion of ending a story with the identical words that the story begins with, their meaning totally opposite.

As far as I recall, this was the only time I ever did it.

Writers like to experiment with structure. An example: a half-hour western I wrote for the series *Lawman*. The title of the story was "Thirty Minutes" and, of course, the story took place in thirty minutes.

Another aspect of "Mirror Mirror . . ." I rarely indulged in was telling a story by having it recounted by a narrator who has no personal involvement in the described events.

Fun if you can make it work.

TWO O'CLOCK SESSION was, as I indicated, part of an anthology in which a number of writers including myself took a shot at attempting to write a "Bradburyesque" type story.

I doubt if any of us managed to equal the quality of Ray's writings. We tried though. The homage was well-intentioned and admiring if far less than the work of the writer we all admire so much.

AND IN SORROW has been published in a "chapbook" by Gauntlet Press—as has "The Prisoner."

Once more, no recollection exists as to when or where the ideas occurred to me.

I hope they are good stories. At the time I wrote them, no magazine cared to purchase them.

Finally though, they are in print, and, I trust, enjoyable to their readers.

LIFE SIZE is a profile in madness. Reg is losing his mind. His first wife, Sally, is dead and he deeply mourns her. He

172   RICHARD MATHESON

identifies with his child and her playmates. His new wife makes demands on him that he can't fulfill. Reg can no longer function. He's cracking up.

ALWAYS BEFORE YOUR VOICE I wrote in 1955 when my family and I were renting a house in Sound Beach on Long Island.

In between descending to the cellar each morning to describe the adventures of my shrinking man, I wrote this story, imagining the mental distress of the postmistress in the small town square who treated me so nicely and knew, I think, that I was a writer.

I have not written very many "straight" short stories but I am glad I wrote this one. I like it very much.

I hope you did as well.

Listening Log

- Every bit of music in your day.

- What was it?
- How did you encounter it?
- Were you listening or hearing it?

CPSIA information can be obtained
at www.ICGtesting.com
Printed in the USA
BVHW081330220720
584347BV00004B/323

9 781943 910649